Magkasintahan
Volume XI

Ukiyoto Publishing

All global publishing rights are held by

Ukiyoto Publishing

Published in 2023

Content Copyright © Ukiyoto
ISBN 9789360166182

All rights reserved.
No part of this publication may be reproduced, transmitted, or stored in a retrieval system, in any form by any means, electronic, mechanical, photocopying, recording or otherwise, without the prior permission of the publisher.

The moral rights of the author have been asserted.

This is a work of fiction. Names, characters, businesses, places, events, locales, and incidents are either the products of the author's imagination or used in a fictitious manner. Any resemblance to actual persons, living or dead, or actual events is purely coincidental.

This book is sold subject to the condition that it shall not by way of trade or otherwise, be lent, resold, hired out or otherwise circulated, without the publisher's prior consent, in any form of binding or cover other than that in which it is published.

www.ukiyoto.com

"It was I who was conquered. In just seven nights, that fledgling goddess not only discovered that I had a heart, but she stole it forever, then cradled it in the palm of her hand."

— *Celeste Bradley, A Courtesan's Guide to Getting Your Man*

Contents

Short Story by Triscia Mae Abe	1
Poems by Maria Cristina Gornez	41
Short Story by Bhon Gloy Jayn P. Cabilete	46
Poems by Chantel Ruecille C. Bargamento	67
Short Story by Golden Rose	102
Short Story by Arius Lauren Raposas	145
Short Story by Jade Alipoon	203
Short Stories and Poem by Czarina Vaneza O. Dungca	212
Poems by Marjorie Sirah San Miguel	249
About the Authors	*257*

Short Story by
Triscia Mae Abe

Psst...I Love You

What is love? Iyan ang parati kong tinatanong sa mga taong nakaranas na no'n. They answered differently like, love is blind, love is about acceptance at ika rin ng iba ang love raw ay masarap sa pakiramdam. They say that love can make a person happy but they're all wrong, because base on my experience, love hurts.

Kung talagang masarap sa pakiramdam ang pagmamahal at magiging masaya ka sa oras na iyon ay iyong maramdaman…bakit naghiwalay ang aking mga magulang? Bakit palagi silang nagtatalo at nag-aaway sa aking harapan? Akala ko ba masaya ang magmahal? Namulat ako sa mundo na iyon ang palaging nasasaksihan. Sigawan dito, sigawaan doon. Ganiyan ba ang pagmamahal?

I never experience love, at wala akong balak na maranasan iyon lalo na't ang madilim na bahagi nito ang aking kinamulatan. My friends called me bitter for saying walang forever and negative words against love pero hindi nila ako masisisi, ganito na talaga ako e.

"Earth to Haven!" sigaw ng isang boses dahilan para mapabalik ako sa aking huwisyo.

Kinunotan ko ng noo ang aking kaibigan na si Lovely at kalauna'y inismiran ito.

"Oh? Anong problema mo?" walang ganang tanong ko.

"Ikaw! Ikaw ang problema ko," singhal nito.

"Ano na naman ba ang ginawa ko sa 'yo? Sa pagkakatanda ko kasi wala e,"

"Kanina pa kasi ako daldal nang daldal dito tapos ikaw nakatanaw lang pala sa malayo. Nasaan na naman ba ang utak mo? Lumipad na naman ba o sumakabilang baryo?" inis na wika nito dahilan para mahina akong mapatawa.

"Sorry na, hindi lang kasi ako interesado sa sinasabi mo," wika ko at mahigpit na niyakap ito.

Nagpakawala naman ito ng malalim na hininga at niyakap din ako. Lovely and I, are childhood friends. Madalas kaming magkasama at magkasundo sa lahat ng bagay pero noong nagkaroon ito ng kasintahan ay para na lamang akong palamuti sa buhay nito.

"Ano pa nga ba? Mag boyfriend ka na rin kasi ng malaman mo ang sinasabi ko," pangungulit nito na siyang kinasira ng mukha ko.

Mabilis pa sa alas kwatrong lumayo ako rito at pabirong niyakap ang aking sarili na para bang natatakot.

"Kilabotan ka nga sa mga sinasabi mo Lovely! Kadiri!" singhal ko na siyang kinabagsak ng panga nito. "At isa pa, ano makukuha ko sa boyfriend na 'yan ha? Hindi ba't sakit lamang sa ulo at puso? Tapos ano? Masasaktan ako? Iiyak din kagaya mo? Ayaw ko nga! Ang saya kayang maging single."

Bagsak balikat akong tiningnan ni Lovely at sinabing, "Grabe, Hindi ko na talaga kinakaya ang pagiging ampalaya mo Haven!"

"Like wise lang gaga!" singhal ko at bahagya pang tumawa. "Hindi ko rin kinakaya ang pagiging love sick fool mo 'no! At isa pa, daig niyo pang dalawa ng boyfriend mo ang aso't pusa kung mag-away tapos maghihiwalay, magbabati ulit tapos away na naman? Kung ako sa'yo Lovely, hihiwalayan ko na 'yan. Balita ko may nilalandi 'yang jowa mo sa kabilang campus," umiiling-iling na dagdag ko.

"Kahit ganiyan kami ng boyfriend ko at least masaya kaming dalawa and that's important! Saang lupalop mo naman nahagip ang balitang iyan aber?" nakapamewang nitong tanong.

"Happy and important my ass…" bulong ko ngunit mukhang narinig nito.

"So?" taas kilay nitong wika.

"Masaya ka naman no'ng wala kang boyfriend ah?"

"Oo, pero ibang kasiyahan ang tinutukoy ko. Huwag mo akong sisimulan Haven Reyes. Ikaw nga riyan walang boyfriend, hindi pa masaya." wika nito na siyang aking kinanganga.

Lovely and I often quarrel about love. At kulang na lamang ay magsapakan na kaming dalawa dahil ni isa sa amin ay walang sumusuko kahit na nalilihis kami minsan sa pinag-uusapan at minsan din ay napupunta na sa personalan pero kahit na ganon ay matibay pa rin ang aming samahan.

"Oh bakit ka namemersonal? Friendship over na tayong dalawa! Hindi na kita bati," tila bata kong wika at tumalikod pa.

"Friendship over mo mukha mo. Ako na nga lang ang nag-iisang kaibigan mo ginaganiyan mo pa ako," saad nito at kinurot ang tagiliran ko dahilan para ako ay mapadaing.

Kahit kailan talaga ay napakasadista ng isang 'to. Maliit lang si Lovely kaya madali at puwedeng-puwede ko I-sako kapag napuno na ako.

"Bakit ka nakangisi? Anong iniisip mo?' tanong ni Lovely na nasa harapan ko na pala.

Pabiro kong nilamusak ang mukha nito at agad na lumabas ng canteen dahil dalawang minuto na lamang ay tutunog na ang bell, hudyat na magsisimula na naman ang aming klase at ang aming paghihirap.

Walang lingon-lingon kong tinungo ang aming silid aralan without minding Lovely's whereabout. Panigurado naman kasing makikipaglampungan pa 'yon at iyon ang ayaw na ayaw kong makita dahil baka masuka lamang ako sa kanilang harapan.

"Oh Haven, bakit nakabusangot ka na naman?" salubong sa akin ng aming class president na si Marissa.

"Nakabusangot ako kasi nakita kita," sagot ko at nilampasan ito.

Mabilis kong tinungo ang aking puwesto sa likurang bahagi ng aming silid aralan at mabilis akong naupo sa upoan ko roon. At bakit nga ba ako nasa likuran? Ang sagot diyan ay simple lang, iyon ay dahil may pagkakataon akong makatulog at kumain ng hindi nila nahuhuli.

Ako si Haven Reyes, twenty-one years old and a Bachelor of Science in Criminology student. At kung itatanong niyo kung bakit ako magpu-pulis? Hindi ko rin alam kung bakit. But so far, so good. I learned a lot about Crimes, Criminals, and Criminology itself. Marami nga lang terminologies at theories na lubhang nakakalito, minsan na nga akong nakakuha ng zero sa pagsusulit namin nang dahil na rin sa kapabayaan at katangahan ko.

I am currently second year at ako lamang ang nagpapa-aral sa aking sarili dahil wala na akong aasahan sa mga magulang ko.

Matagal na akong nawalan ng magulang magmula noong nagloko ang tatay ko na siyang sinundan naman ng nanay ko. I sometimes wonder kung nagkamali ba sa pagpana si Kupido dahil hindi naman naging masaya ang mga magulang ko kagaya ng tinutukoy ng iba at laman ng libro.

They said that, marriage is sacred. Then why did they cheat? Sagrado pala pero bakit nila iyon sinisira, binabalewala at dinudungisan? Hindi ba nila alam na hindi lang sila ang maaapektuhan sa bawat desisyon na kanilang ginagawa? Why are they so eager to taste different dish when they're already committed and married? Edi sana hindi sila nagpakasal sa gayon ay walang maaapektuhan at walang masisirang kinabukasan.

After a few more minutes ay dumating na ang professor namin sa Forensic Science na si Sir Ramos and as usual, wala pa rin si Lovely at paniguradong ako na naman ang gigisahin ng isang 'to.

"Miss Reyes," pagtawag nito sa akin na siyang inaasahan ko.

"Yes Sir?" tugon ko.

"Where is your friend?" taas kilay nitong tanong.

I just shrug my shoulders and open my notes like nothing happened. Kahit naman magpaliwanag ako rito ay wala pa ring magbabago, late pa rin si Lovely at palaging damay ako.

"Tell your friend to meet me at the detention room," mariing wika nito. "Now stand up and answer my question."

"Yes Sir,"

Labag man sa aking kalooban ay tumayo na ako, palagi naman kasing ganito. Kasalanan ng isa, kasalanan ng lahat at talagang namumuro na ang pinakamamahal kong kaibigan.

"What is crime scene?" seryoso nitong tanong.

Nagpakawala muna ako ng isang malalim na hininga at sinalubong ang nakakamatay nitong tingin.

"Crime scene is the treasure island of investigators because they can find all the evidences there,"

Tumango ito sa aking naging tugon kaya ako ay nakahinga ng maluwag.

"Why do criminals goes back to the crime scene?"

"Well Sir, base on my opinion, criminals goes back to the crime scene or crime place to make sure that they doesn't leave evidences behind that can identify them or point them during the investigation."

"Well said, Miss Reyes. Now take your sit and let's proceed on our discussion," wika nito at mabilis naman sa alas kwatrong ako ay umupo.

During the discussion I am pre-occupied. Lumulipad na naman ang aking isipan mabuti na lamang talaga at hindi na ako tinatawag at pinapansin ni Sir. Forensic Science is one of my favorite subjects pero ngayon ay wala talaga ako sa mood na makinig.

What is love? Base on the internet, Love is a set of emotion and behaviors characterized by intimacy, passion, and commitment. It also associated with a range of positive emotions, including happiness, excitement, life satisfaction, and euphoria, but it can also result in negative emotions such as jealousy and stress. In short, love is complicated. And I hate complicated things that's why I hate love.

Nayayamot akong napatayo at napakamot ng aking ulo nang mapagtantong nag-iisa na lang pala ako sa loob ng aming classroom. Malamang ay nagsi-uwian na ang mga classmates ko para maghanda. Iisa lang ang subject namin ngayong araw dahil mayroong event sa main campus at base kay Sir Ramos, kailangan naming pumunta dahil mandatory iyon.

"Panibagong gastos na naman," mahina kong bulong habang naglalakad.

Ako ay nag-aaral sa isang kilalang paaralan, which is the TMCA Colleges. TMCA Colleges have different branches all over the Philippines pero mas kilala pa rin talaga ang main campus nito na matatagpuan sa Antipolo City na bahagyang may kalayoan sa bahay ko.

Tahimik kong tinatahak ang daan papauwi sa aming munting tahanan. Ako ay nakatira sa San Ildefonso, Bulacan, at humigit kumulang dalawang oras ang gugugolin ko sa byahe kung pupunta ako ng Antipolo pero kung traffic naman ay baka abotin ako ng gabi. Mabuti na lamang at may tutuloyan ako sa Antipolo dahil naroroon ang ibang mga kamag-anak ko.

Hindi pa man ako nakakapasok ng aming bahay ay rinig na rinig ko na ang sigawan ng aking mga magulang at ganon rin ang bulongan ng aming mga chismosang kapitbahay. Sa araw-araw na ginawa ng Diyos, wala silang ibang ginawa kundi ang mag-away at magsigawan. Tila ba'y mayroong speaker ang lalamunan ng mga ito.

"Masaya ba ang palabas?" tanong ko dahilan para mapabaling sa akin ang atensiyon ng lahat.

"Oo Haven! Lalo na ngayong may bago na namang isyu ang magaling mong Nanay," natatawang sagot ng isa dahilan para mangunot ang aking noo.

"Isyu?" nagugulohang tanong ko.

"Oo, kabit daw kasi ng kumpare ng Tatay mo ang Nanay mo! Ang galing 'di ba? Daig pa ang teleserye," wika nito dahilan para manlaki ang mga mata ko.

Mabilis at padarag akong pumasok sa aming bahay at labis akong nadismaya sa aking nasaksihan. Ang nanay ko ay may magulong buhok, nagdurugo rin ang labi nito at umiiyak. Samantalang ang tatay ko naman ay puno ng kalmot ang buong mukha.

"Anong nangyayari rito?" seryosong tanong ko.

"Itong Nanay mo kasi Haven, may ginawa na namang katarantaduhan!" sigaw ng aking Ama habang nakatiim bagang.

"Wala akong ginagawang masama!" sigaw naman ng aking Ina.

"Maryro'n! Huwag ka ng magmaang-maangan pa Hannah! Kitang-kita ng dalawa kong mga mata kung paano kayo naghalikan ni Patrick!" nangagalaiting sigaw ng Ama ko.

At bago pa man sila muling magkasakitan ay gumitna na ako at napabuntong hininga.

"Ma, Pa, puwede bang tama na?" mahina ngunit mariin kong wika. "Hindi na po ba talaga kayo marunong mahiya? Kanina pa kayo pinagpi-pyestahan ng mga kapitbahay natin sa labas. Kung hindi kayo nahihiya p'wes ako, oo! Hindi ba't hiwalay na naman kayo? May kaniya-kaniya na kayong pamilya hindi ba? Pero bakit ako pa rin ang ginugulo niyo? Bakit sa tuwing may problema o alitan kayo ako palagi ang iniipit niyo?" dugtong ko pa ngunit sa kabila ng hinanaing ko ay tanging malakas na sampal lamang ang natanggap ko mula sa Nanay ko.

"Wala kang karapatang pagsalitaan ako ng ganiyan Haven! Tandaan mo, anak lang kita. Kung hindi dahil sa akin ay patay ka na. Manang-mana ka talaga sa Tatay mong bastardo, parehas kayong masama ang ugali at patapon!" galit na sigaw nito at binangga pa ang balikat ko bago tuloyang lumabas ng bahay na siyang sinundan naman ng Tatay ko.

Nanlulumo akong napaupo sa sahig ng aming bahay na kung saan ako na lamang ang nakatira. Pumupunta lamang silang dalawa rito hindi upang mangamusta kundi upang mag-away.

My parent's often do physical fight at minsan din ay nadadamay ako sa away nilang 'yon. Kamuntik na rin akong kunin ng DSWD sa kanila ngunit pinili ko pa ring manatili dahil mahal ko silang pareho kahit na hindi nila ako mahal. At the young age my parents abandoned me pero palagi kong sinasabi sa aking sarili na in the end of the day, and in the end of every fight they are still my parents.

Mabilis kong tinuyo ang luhang dumaloy sa aking mga mata. Ang sabi ko hindi na ako iiyak nang dahil sa kanila pero wala e, sadyang masakit talaga ang maabandona. My parents are both happy in their new family, why me? I am miserable as always.

How can they smile, laugh and sleep at night without getting guilt for abandoning their child? O, baka naman talaga sa una pa lamang ay hindi na nila ako ginusto. Then, why did they named me Haven? Am I a joke to them? Am I a mistake? Or am I adopted?

"Calm down Haven, everything will be alright." pagpapagaan ko sa loob ko.

Wala na akong natitirang kakampi sa mundong ito kundi ang sarili ko. Well, I have Lovely but she's so busy with her boyfriend.

Mapait akong napangiti nang makita ang kabuoan ng bahay. Sobrang magulo iyon at marami ring nagkalat na basag na salamin. Actually inaasahan ko na 'to, ganito naman kasi palagi ang senaryo kapag tapos na silang mag-away at manggulo.

Napasabunot na lamang ako ng aking buhok bago nagsimulang maglinis. Mukhang hindi pa yata ako makakapunta sa event.

"Bahala na si Batman," usal ko at muling bumalik sa paglilinis.

Pagkaraan ng isa't kalahating oras ay tuloyan na rin akong natapos sa paglilinis. At sa loob ng isa't kalahating oras na iyon ay hindi ako namahinga. I love busying myself because by the help of it I can temporarily forgot my problems.

Tinungo ko ang aking munting kuwarto upang magbihis at mamahinga. Wala na akong balak pang pumunta ng Antipolo upang umattend ng event. For sure naman nabalitaan na nila ang nangyari sa akin. Iba na kasi sa panahon ngayon, may pakpak na ang balita.

Kinabukasan ako ay nagising nang dahil sa sobrang sakit ng aking ulo. Mukhang lalagnatin pa yata ako sa araw na ito at iyon ay hindi maaari sapagkat may reporting pa ako at isa pa'y mayroon din akong baho. I have a part-time job at the club near our school, isa akong waitress doon at minsan naman ay kumakanta ako para dagdag kita. Noong kasama ko pa sa bahay ang mga magulang ko ay wala akong naitatabing pera para sa aking sarili dahil madalas nila iyong inuubos at kinukuha.

Mabilis ang aking mga naging pagkilos. Pagkabangon ko ay agad akong naligo at nagbihis, hindi na rin ako nag-abala pang kumain sapagkat malapit na akong malate para sa aking first subject. Labis akong nagpapasalamat na malapit lamang ang TMCA Colleges sa aming bahay kaya kahit papaano ay nakahabol pa ako.

"Okay ka lang? Namumutla ka," tanong sa akin ni Lovely na naririto na pala.

"Himala yata at maaga ka?" wika ko at nginisihan ito.

Awtomatiko namang umikot ang mga mata nito at ako'y inismiran. "Syempre, may usapan kasi kami ng boyfriend ko."

I sulk because of what she said. "Umagang-umaga sinisira mo ang araw ko,"

"Alangan namang gabi mo ang masira ko e, umaga pa lang hindi ba?" sarkasmo nitong saad dahilan para umawang ang labi ko.

"At talagang pinipilosopo mo pa ako?" taas kilay kong tanong. "Baka gusto mong sabihin ko lahat sa 'yo ang mga naging atraso mo sa 'kin?"

"Luh, wala namang ganiyanan Haven. Nagbibiro lang naman ako e, sorry na. I love you best friend," malambing nitong wika at niyakap pa ako.

Naiirita ko naman itong tinulak papalayo. I'm not really a fan of physical touch. I get easily annoyed and pissed when someone touches or hugs me. Hindi ko rin mawari kong bakit, basta hindi ko lang talaga siya bet. Maybe because I never experienced it with my parents.

"Grabe ka na talaga Haven! Makahawi wagas?" inis na wika ni Lovely habang nakatingin sa akin ng masama. At kung nakakamatay lang ang tingin ay paniguradong kanina pa ako nakabulagta.

"Alam mo naman kasing naiirita ako, yumakap ka pa," katwiran ko at nangalumbaba.

"Balita ko may live show sa inyo kahapon?"

"Tama nga iyang nabalitaan mo," saad ko kasabay nang pagpapakawala ng isang malalim na hininga.

"Hindi na talaga nagsasawa at nagbabago iyang mga magulang mo ano?" umiiling-iling na wika nito.

"Hindi na. Tatanda na silang ganiyan,"

"Kamusta ka naman?" tanong nito at kung may anong mainit na bagay ang humaplos sa puso ko.

Kahit malandi at puro pag-ibig ang nag-iisang kaibigan ko na 'to, hindi pa rin ito nakakalimot na kamustahin ako at ang nararamdaman ko.

"Well, I can survive. Nasanay na rin ako," balewala kong saad at nagkibit balikat pa.

"Alam mo ba Haven?"

"Hindi ko pa alam," sagot ko habang nakangisi.

"Sira!" singhal nito at kinaltukan ako. "Talagang hindi mo pa alam kasi hindi ko pa sinasabi."

"Ano ba kasi 'yon?" iritado kong tanong.

"Bilib ako sa 'yo," seryosong saad nito.

"Bakit naman?" nagugulohang tanong ko.

Tiningnan ako nito sa aking mga mata dahilan para bahagya akong mangilabot. I am not used to it. Hindi ako sanay na makitang seryoso si Lovely. Sa amin kasing dalawa siya ang pinaka-bubbly.

"Bilib ako sa 'yo kasi nakaya mo ang set-up niyo ng mga magulang mo. Kung ako siguro ikaw, matagal na akong nagpatiwakal o kaya naman sumuko. But you? You're a fighter Haven. Hindi ka sumuko kahit na inuulan ka ng samu't saring problema. Na kahit pilit ka ng isinusuka ng mundo, nariyan ka pa rin, matayog na nakatayo."

"'Wag ka ngang magsalita ng ganiyan Lovely. Kinikilabotan ako e, at isa pa, matagal ko ng alam na isa akong strong independent woman and in additional, maganda rin ako at sexy," nakangisi kong saad.

"Wow ah? Biglang nagbuhat ng sariling bangko. Oo na lang Haven, baka umiyak ka pa,"

Pabiro kong hinampas ito sa balikat at kalaunan ay malakas na napatawa. Kahit papaano ay naging magaan ang aking pakiramdam nang dahil sa sinabi nito. Having Lovely as a friend saves me from harming myself many times.

"Pero alam mo ba Haven? Nakita ko siya," bulong nito sa aking tainga.

"Who?" kunot noo kong tanong.

"Iyong childhood crush nating dalawa, si Dazed."

"Dazed who? Hindi ko 'yan kilala,"

"Weh? Talaga ba? Parang dati lang iniyakan mo siya kasi nagkaroon ng girlfriend 'di ba?"

"Wala akong iniyakan 'no!" singhal ko at labis akong nagpapasalamat ng dumating na ang aming guro.

Dazed Scott is indeed my childhood crush. Anak ito ng mayor namin sa Bulacan. Pogi, moreno, may mapupungay na mga mata, makakapal na kilay, matangkad, at mayaman, at halos nasa kaniya na ang lahat kaya nga hindi kami bagay. Dazed is a graduating student with a engineering course at ayon sa mga nasasagap kong balita ay papalit-palit daw ito ng kasintahan. Mga lalaki nga naman.

I liked him because he's kind at hanggang doon na lamang ang paghanga kong iyon sa kadahilanang sinampal niya ako ng katotohanan na masyado pa akong bata para sa kaniya. Na hindi kagaya kong babae ang magugustohan niya and at that young age, I became bitter.

Pagkatapos ng klase ay naghiwalay din agad kami ng landas ni Lovely. Masama pa rin ang aking pakiramdam pero kailangan kong magtrabaho upang may pangtustos ako sa pag-aaral ko.

"Magandang hapon po Kuya," bati ko sa bouncer ng club.

"Magandang hapon din Haven. Ang aga mo yata ngayon? " nakangiti nitong wika.

"Maaga po ako ngayon para makarami. Matagal din po kasi akong nahinto nang dahil sa alam mo na po," magalang kong saad.

"Oh siya, pumasok ka na sa loob at mamahinga ka muna. Bahagya ka kasing namumutla,"

"Opo," wika ko at agad na tinungo ang locker room.

Nagpakawala ako ng isang malalim na hininga at agad na nahiga sa pag-isahang sofa. Nagsiratingan na rin ang iba pang mga working students na kagaya ko at ang iba sa kanila ay mga classmates ko.

"Kanina ka pa ba Haven?" tanong sa akin ni Ate Jana.

"Hindi naman po," sagot ko kasabay ng pag-upo.

"Magbihis ka na, madaming customer ngayon," saad nito habang may tinitingnan na kung ano.

"Opo," sagot ko.

"Siya nga pala,"

"Po?"

"Huwag kang masyadong magpapagod," wika nito na siyang naglagay ng ngiti sa labi ko.

Ate Jana treats me like her own younger sister that warms my heart so much. Mabilis akong nagbihis at agad na nagtungo sa second floor ng club dahil ayon kay Ate Jana ay mas marami raw ang tao roon at kailangan ng maraming waiter at waitresses.

Isang praktisadong ngiti ang iplinastar ko sa aking labi at nagsimula ng magtrabaho. Kung sa unang palapag ay sobrang magulo, iba rito. It looks like a private meeting or party. Mayroon din akong nakikitang mga kilalang personalidad, nakapang office suit, at mga anak politiko.

"Do you think Dazed will come?" rinig kong tanong ng isang babae.

Nakuha niyon ang aking atensyion kaya binagalan ko ang pagsalin ng alak sa kopita ng babae.

"Of course! It's his birthday celebration after all," sagot nito.

Namayani ang katahimikan sa pagitan ng dalawang babae kaya naman ay umalis na ako. Hindi ko mawari pero kinakabahan ako. Ang bilis-bilis din ng tibok ng aking puso, hindi iyon normal kagaya ng aking nakasanayan.

"Ayos ka lang ba Haven?" tanong sa akin ni Vhince. Ang bartender.

"O-Oo, ayos lang ako," nauutal na sagot ko.

"Namumutla ka, magpahinga ka kaya muna?"

"Ano ka ba Vhince, ayos lang ako. Malayo 'to sa bituka," natatawa kong saad at marahang tinapik ito sa balikat.

Ako ay namaalam muna rito upang pumunta ng banyo at sa kalagitnaan ng aking pagliko ay nabangga ako sa isang matigas na bagay at sigurado akong hindi iyon pader dahil iyon ay dumaing.

"Sorry!" singhal ko at mabilis na yumuko. Mahirap na baka isa sa mga bisita 'to.

"Rise your head. It's okay," saad ng isang baritono ngunit malamig na tinig na siyang nagpatindig ng aking mga balahibo.

Hindi ko alam kung saan ko narinig ang boses na 'yon pero iyon ay pamilyar sa aking pandinig.

Nanginginig man ay nag-angat ako ng tingin and my breathing hitch when the man's deep black eyes met my brown ones. Mayroon itong itim na itim ngunit mapupungay na mga mata, matangos ang ilong nito, at ang labi nito ay hugis puso na siyang kinamangha ko. Nakita ko nag pag-angat ng sulok ng labi nito kaya naman mabilis akong nag-iwas ng tingin. Mukhang masyado na akong natagalan sa pagtitig.

"I'm so sorry Sir," paghingi ko ng paumanhin.

"It's okay, kasalanan ko rin naman." wika nito at marahang tinapik ang aking balikat dahilan para ako ay mapaigtad.

Mabilis akong lumayo sa lalaki nang dahil sa kakaibang init at elektrisidad na aking naramdaman sa kabuoan ng aking katawan.

"A-ahm, una na po ako Sir," aligaga kong saad at nilampasan ito.

Lakad takbo ang aking ginawa at nanghihinang napasandal ako sa marmol na dingding ng banyo habang sapo-sapo ang aking dibdib. Kahit namumutla at nanghihina ay ramdam ko ang pang-iinit ng magkabilaan kong pisngi.

"Haven anong nangyayari sa 'yo?" tanong ko sa aking sarili.

Mabilis kong tinungo ang sink at makailang beses akong naghilamos ngunit kahit ilang beses ko na iyong ginawa ay hindi pa rin nababawasan ang init ng aking mukha. I feel like I got enchanted at first sight.

Marahan kong tinapik ang aking magkabilaang pisgi bago tuloyang lumabas ng banyo at sa aking paglabas ay muli akong nanigas ng bumulaga sa akin ang lalaking nakabanggaan ko kani-kanina lang.

"M-May kailangan po kayo Sir?" magalang na tanong ko.

"Meron," walang ngiting tugon nito.

"Ano po 'yon? Puwede po ba tayong lumipat ng puwesto? Nakaharang po kasi tayo sa pasilyo ng banyo,"

"Okay. Lead the way," the man said.

Kagaya nga ang sinabi nito ay nauna na ako. Kahit kabado ay nagawa ko pa rin itong ngitian kahit na papaano.

"Dito na tayo Sir," saad ko ng nakarating na kami sa veranda. "Ano po ang kailangan mo sa akin?" dugtong ko pa.

I heard the man heave a sigh then chuckles making my forehead creased.

"It's been a while Haven..." mahinang wika nito na siyang mas kinakunot ng noo ko.

"How did you know my name?" puno ng pagtataka kong tanong. "Oh, I have name plate nga pala. Silly me," natatwa kong dugtong.

"Kahit hindi ako tumingin sa name plate mo kilala na kita. Kahit nakatalikod ka pa, kilala kita Haven," nakangiti nitong wika.

"Sino ka ba talaga?" tiim bagang kong tanong. "Wala akong oras makipaglaokohan sa 'yo."

"Dazed Scott. Ang lalaking pinangakoan mo ng kasal,"

Pabaling-baling ako sa aking higaan. Kanina pa ako nakauwi pero hindi pa rin ako makatulog. Ilang beses na rin akong nagbilang ng mga tupa, kumanta na rin ako pero wala iyong naging talab at iyon ay kasalanan lahat ni Dazed at ng mga katagang binitawan niya.

"Ano ba ang nangyayari sa 'yo Haven? Kumalma ka nga para kang tanga," kastigo ko sa aking sarili.

Muli akong nagpakawala ng sa malalim na hininga at bumangon mula sa aking pagkakahiga. Kinuha ko ang aking selpon at binuksan ang aking social media and to my surprise I have a new friend request. Agad ko iyong pinindot at ako ay napatigal-gal ng aking makita ang pangalan ni Dazed.

Walang pagdadalawang isip kong binura ang friend request nito at muli na lamang akong nahiga sa munti kong kama and to my shock I feel into a deep slumber.

Ako ay nagising nang dahil sa nakakabinging katok mula sa pinto ng aking bahay at pakiramdam ko ay masisira nito ang pintong iyon. Nayayamot man ay tumayo ako. Hindi na ako naghilamos o kung ano pa man dahil wala ako sa mood at isa pa hindi naman siguro artista ang bubulaga sa 'kin pagbukas ko ng pinto.

"Sandali!" malakas na sigaw ko. "Makakatok naman 'to wagas." bulong ko pa.

Sa pagbukas ko ng pintoan ay isang pumpon ng bulaklak ang bumulaga sa akin. Niinis ko iyong hinawi na siya ring agad kong pinagsisihan dahil bumungad sa akin ang mukha ni Dazed na may malawak na ngiti sa labi.

"Good morning Haven," bati nito habang nakangiti.

"Anong ginagawa mo rito?" nanlalaking mga matang tanong ko.

"I am here to court you just like I promised ten years ago,"

"Nagbibiro ka ba?" tumatawang tanong ko rito.

Dazed eyes me seriously making me choke in nervousness.

"Hindi ako nagbibiro Haven. I'm always serious when it comes to you,"

Marahan akong pumalakpak nang dahil sa sinabi nito. "Talaga lang ah? Nice try but you can't fool me. I know you very well, Dazed."

"I see...your still holding grudge on me," Dazed said then sigh.

"Mabuti naman at alam mo," puno ng pang-uuyam na saad ko.

"Look, Haven. I'm sorry okay? Alam kong mali ang ginawa ko ilang taon na ang nakakaraan pero, I just did that because you're too young for me at ayaw ko namang angkinin ka sa murang edad," wika nito na puno ng pagsusumamo.

"Really? Do I look like I care?" puno ng sarkasmo kong saad at pinagsarhan ito ng pinto.

Sabado ngayon at ang buong araw ko ay sirang-sira na nang dahil sa Dazed na iyon. Makailang beses pa itong kumatok sa pinto at tinawag ang aking pangalan na siyang hindi ko na lamang pinansin dahil mas lalo lamang akong maiirita.

Ano nga ba ang nangyari ilang taon na ang nakakaraan? Well, this is what happened. The young me confesses her feelings to Dazed at ano pa nga ba ang aasahan? Syempre pinagtawanan lamang ako nito. I really like Dazed and I can't deny the fact that he have special spot in my heart kaya nga palagi akong inaasar ni Lovely dahil alam nitong may nararamdaman pa rin ako.

Noong bagong salta pa lamang dito si Dazed ay nakuha na nito ang buo kong atensyon at pagkatao. I am a die hard fan girl of him at minsan na rin akong naging stalker nito nang dahil sa labis na paghanga.

"Ang lakas naman ng tama ng isang 'yon," naiiling kong wika habang nagluluto.

Hindi ko alam kung nakaalis na ba si Dazed o hindi pa, pero base sa katahimikang namumutawi masasabi kong ito ay nakauwi na ngunit ako ay nagkamali dahil ng napabaling ang aking atensyon sa bintana ay malakas akong napasigaw ng makira ko roon si Dazed na nakadungaw.

"Anak ng pating!" nanlalaking mga matang sigaw ko at agad itong nilapitan. "Anong ginagawa mo riyan?" tanong ko pa.

"Hello there my beautiful future wife," nakangiti nitong saad. "Naririto ako upang masilayan ang magandang mukha ng mapapangasawa ko."

"Tigilan mo nga ako!" singhal ko at inirapan ito kahit sa totoo niyan ay bahagyang kinikilig ako.

Damn this man. He never fails to give me butterflies in my stomach and make my heart flutter.

"Hinding-hindi kita titigilan Haven ko," malamyos na wika nito na siyang kinanganga ko.

"Saan mo naman natutunan 'yan Dazed freaking Scott? Hindi bagay! Maghunos-dili ka nga," kunsome kong wika.

Totoo naman kasing hindi bagay rito ang gano'ng uri ng pananalita. Ang jejemon masyado, parang iyong mga tambay na palamunin na nasa kanto.

"Well, you're right my wife. My wife sounds better than Haven ko thou," saad nito at kinindatan pa ako.

Hindi ko na lamang ito pinansin at muli na lamang bumalik sa pagluluto. Kahit nakatalikod ay ramdam na ramdam ko ang mainit na pagtitig ni Dazed. It's kind of making me uncomfortable but still I didn't mind it kasi malayo naman ito sa akin.

I heave a sigh then looks at Dazed direction. Lihim akong napangiti ng makita ang itsura nito. Para itong batang nakasilip sa munting siwang ng bintana ko.

"Stop staring will you?" pagsusuplada ko rito.

"I can't help it. You look beautiful and hot while cooking my wife," wika nito habang nakangiti.

Mariin kong kinagat ang aking pang-ibabang labi upang maitago ang aking ngiting pilit na kumakawala. "Huwag mo nga akong binobola!"

"I'm not! Nagasasabi ako ng totoo," seryosong saad nito.

"Oo na nga lang. Umalis ka na nga," pagtataboyan ko rito.

"I don't wanna. I want to watch you a little longer,"

"You're creepy,"

"I'm not. It's just that I've missed you so much Haven. I regret moving away. Nagsisisi akong lumuwas pa ako edi sana masaya ka na ngayon sa piling ko," saad nito na siyang kinanganga ko.

"Ang kapal naman yata ng mukha mo Mister Dazed?" hindi makapaniwalang wika ko.

"Indeed, I have a handsome face. Thank you so much for that complement my wife,"

Nagpakawala na lamang ako ng isang malalim na hininga nang dahil sa kahanginan nito. Hindi ito ang Dazed na hinangaan ko. Ibang-iba ito sa Dazed na kinalakihan ko at sa Dazed na laman ng mga balita.

"Ikaw ba talaga si Dazed? " hindi mapigilang tanong ko.

"I am," tugon nito.

"Hindi ako naniniwala. Ang Dazed na kilala at nakagisnan ko ay masungit hindi ganiyan magsalita at higit sa lahat ay hindi ako gusto," seryosong saad ko.

Dazed heave a sigh the ruffles his dark black shiny hair. He look so handsome while doing that. I even see rays of the sun shining in his back.

"It's me, Dazed. At tanging sa 'yo lamang ako ganito. I am so tired hiding my real feelings for you. I am so tired pretending that you're just nobody. I am so sick of those fake love that I had just to forget about you. I want to be the real me in front of you Haven. I am always like this but It looks like you can't see the real me because of your grudge," namumungay na mga matang saad nito.

It somewhat pains me hearing Dazed say those words. Siguro ay tama nga ito, na nang dahil sa galit na nararamdaman ko ay hindi ko na matukoy kung alin ang totoo.

"If you really love me then why did your father approved my parents annulment?' tiim bagang kong tanong.

I saw how Dazed get stunned because of my question making me smile bitterly. Hindi lang naman kasi ang pagtawa nito sa pag-amin ko ang problema. The other problem is that, his father approved the annulment of my parents. He saw me that time, begging to his father to not approve the annulment pero wala siyang ginawa. Hinayaan niya lamang akong umiyak doon at mapahiya. Iyan ba ang sinasabi niyang mahal niya ako?

"It's for your own good too Haven. Alam ko ang sitwasyon mo at kung ano ang ginagawa sa 'yo ng mga magulang mo kaya wala akong ginawa para pigilan ang Papa ko. Because what he did is right. Tama lamang na inaprobahan nito ang annulment dahil kung hindi, mas lalala pa ang problema at mas mahihirapan, maiipit at masasaktan ka at ayaw kong mangyari ang bagay na iyon," Dazed said seriously while staring straight into my eyes.

Ayaw ko mang aminin pero tama Si Dazed. Siguro kung hindi pa hiwalay ang mga magulang ko paniguradong mas naghihirap ako ngayon ng husto. Or maybe, I already died because of physical abuse and starving.

"Umalis ka na." walang emosyon kong saad.

"Ayaw," tila bata nitong saad at ngumuso pa.

Nagpakawala na lamang ako ng malalim na hininga at naghanda na lamang upang makakain na. Habang kumakain ay hindi ko maiwasang mailang dahil katapat ko si Dazed na nasa bintana pa rin. Para itong batang namamalimos nang dahil sa posisyon namin.

"Ano pa ba kasi ang kailangan mo sa 'kin?" iritado kong tanong.

"Wala naman, gusto lang talaga kitang masilayan. Seeing your face makes me feel at ease and safe,"

"At ngayong nakita mo na ang mukha ko, puwede ka na naman na sigurong umalis hano?" taas kilay na saad ko.

"Depende," Dazed saids while shrugging his broad shoulders.

"Depende sa?" tanong ko at binitawan ang kubyertos na aking hawak.

"Depende kung maririnig ko mula sa labi mo na mahal mo rin ako," saad nito na siyang kinatigil ko.

"Ang kapal naman ng mukha mo!" singhal ko dahilan para malakas na mapatawa ito.

"Just say it Haven. I will catch you this time," pamimilit nito.

"Paano kaya kung suntokin ko 'yang pagmumukha mo?" pananakot ko dahilan para mapalunok ito ng mariin.

Inirapan ko na lamang ito at muli na lamang bumalik sa pagkain.

"Psst!" sitsit nito na siyang hindi ko pinansin.

"Psst Haven!" ulit nito.

Nagpakawala na lamang ako ng isang malalim na hininga at ito'y tinalikuran.

"Sungit naman ng wifey ko na 'yan,"

"Tigilan mo nga ako!" singhal ko.

"Hinding-hindi kita titigilan sapagkat ikaw ang isinisigaw ng puso ko,"

"Kwento mo sa pagong," panunuya ko na siyang kinatawa nito.

Hearing Dazed laugh makes my heart beats fast. Nasapo ko ang aking dibdib nang dahil sa pagtawang ginawa nito. Pakiramdam ko ay malalagutan ako ng hininga nang dahil sa sobrang kilig na aking nadarama.

"Psst!"

"Ano ba?!" iritadong sigaw ko at muli itong hinarap.

"I love you," seryoso nitong wika at ako'y kinindatan.

Ang pag-inog ng aking mundo ay huminto. I can't breathe properly and my heart is beating wildly. Nanlalaki lamang ang aking mga mata habang nakatitig sa maamo nitong mukha. I can't utter a single word. I'm in total shock.

"Hindi ako naghihintay ng tugon Haven, pero umaasa ako na ganon din ang nararamdaman mo. Ngayong nasabi ko na sa 'yo ang nararamdaman ko ay nakahinga na rin ako sa wakas ng maluwag. I love you Haven. I really do. You're my dream that I can't reach even though your not that far away. I love you so much and it hurts," wika nito at iniwanan ang bulaklak sa bintana.

Saka lamang ako nakahinga ng maluwag ng ito ay nawala na sa aking paningin. Ako ay tumayo at inabot ang bulaklak at bahagya iyong inamoy.

"I love you too Dazed, but unlike you, I don't have a guts." bulong ko.

Kinabukasan ay sinalubong ako ng nakakarinding tinig ni Lovely.

"Ano ba ang nangyayari sa 'yo ha?" salubong kilay na tanong ko.

"Wala naman Haven. Kinikilig lang ako," saad nito at hinampas pa ang balikat ko.

"At bakit ka naman kinikilig aber?"

"Ay hindi mo alam?" gulantang nitong tanong.

"Tatanongin ba kita kung alam ko?" pamimilosopo ko.

"Sabi ko nga,' pagsuko nito. "Ganito kasi 'yan Haven. May nakakita kay Dazed na bumili ng bulaklak at nagtungo sa inyo at narinig pa ang confession ni Dazed sa 'yo. Sabi ko na nga ba't gusto ka rin ng isang 'yon!"

Nanlalaking mga matang tinitigan ko ang aking kaibigan. Hindi ko lubos maisip na may makakaalam agad sa nangyari. Sabagay ano pa nga ba ang aasahan ko? Isang kilalang tao si Dazed at kahit saan ito magpunta ay may mga matang nakasunod dito.

"So kayo na?" taas babang kilay na tudyo nito.

"Hindi," tugon ko at naupo na sa aking upoan.

Ramdam ko ang malisyosong titig ng aking mga kamag-aral gayon din ang kanilang nakakamatay na pagtitig na siyang ipinagsawalang bahala ko na lamang.

"What?!" malaks na sigaw ni Lovely dahilan para ako ay mapaigtad.

"Kumalma ka nga!" singhal ko.

"Sa palagay mo paano ako kakalma? Gaga ka talaga Haven! Manok na nga ang llumalapit sa 'yo tinaboy mo pa," eksaherada nitong wika.

"So?"

"So ka riyan!" singhal nito at ako ay inakbayan. "Alam ko namang mahal mo rin si Dazed, bakit hindi mo subokan? Malay mo siya na pala iyong the one. Iyong lalaking magpapabago ng mindset mo about love. Iyong lalaking magpaparamdam sa 'yo kung ano nga ba ang pagmamahal na hindi mo naramdaman sa mga magulang mo. Huwag kang mag-alala Haven, naririto lang ako para sa 'yo at kung sasaktan ka man ni Dazed, magtago na siya dahil babalatan ko siya ng buhay."

Natatawang ginulo ko ang buhok ni Lovely at nanatiling tahimik na lamang. Paano nga kaya kung subokan ko? Gusto kong subokan pero natatakot ako na baka sa huli ay masaktan lamang ako.

I'm used of pain pero ibang sakit pa rin talaga ang hatid ng pag-ibig at pagmamahal.

I want to experience love on it's finest. Iyong tipong hindi ako masasaktan at luluha nang dahil sa desisyon kong magmahal. I want to experience pure love, no judgement, just acceptance.

I want to met a man that will love me like how God loves us. I want to be love by a man that can accept my flaws and imperfections. I want to be with a man that can accept me for who I am.

I am a sucker for happy ever after na siyang hindi ko nasaksihan sa aking mga magulang. Pilit ko itanggi at itago ang aking tunay na nararamdaman ay pili pa ring itong kumakawala. I am hopelessly in love with the man named Dazed Scott.

Dazed will be forever my childhood crush and puppy love. I'm admiring him ever since we met. The way his black eyes sparkles when he's happy makes my day. The way he smiles eases the pain that I am feeling every time my mother and father are arguing.

"Tulala ka na naman," bulong ni Lovely sa akin.

Ito ay binalingan ko ng tingin at tinaasan ng kilay. "Bakit? May kailangan ka na naman ba?"

"Wala naman, concern lang ako sa 'yo kasi lumilipad na naman ang diwa mo," pang-aasar nito.

"Paano kaya kung isumbong kita kay Sir na hindi ka na naman gumawa ng crime maping report?" pananakot ko na siyang kinaputla nito.

"Huwag ka namang ganiyan Haven! Parang hindi tayo magkaibigan ah? But speaking of Sir, nasaan na kaya iyon at hanggang ngayon ay wala pa? Hindi naman nahuhuli 'yon ah?" wika nito na siyang pinagtataka ko rin.

Isang malakas na katok mula sa pintuan ng aming classroom ang pumukaw sa aming atensyon. Iyon ay binalingan namin ng tingin at ang mata ko'y lumuwa ng aking makita si Dazed na may malawak na ngiti sa labi.

"Oh my ghad…" rinig kong bulong ni Lovely.

My eyes didn't leave Dazed every single steps. Nakasunod ang aking mga mata sa bawat paghakbang nitong ginagawa hanggang sa ito ay huminto sa gitna at ako'y mariing napalunok ng magtama ang aming mga mata.

I saw how a sly smile formed on Dazed lips na siyang kinasama ng timpla ng aking mukha.

"Good morning everyone, I am Dazed Scott and I will be your teacher for the mean time," seryosong saad nito na siyang kinabunyi ng mga classmates ko. Lalo na ng mga babae na siyang kinairap ko.

"Ang pogi naman talaga ni Fafa Dazed," kinikilig na bulong sa akin ni Lovely.

"Tumigil ka nga! Para kang kiti-kiti," suway ko rito.

"Before we start, may gusto ba kayong itanong?" saad ni Dazed na nakatitig pa rin sa akin.

"Kung ice cream ka lang siguro Haven, tunaw ka na." pang-aasar ni Lovely na siyang kinapula ng aking mukha.

Ito ay siniko ko para tumigil pero mas lalo lamang itong lumala. Nagsimula ng magtanong ang mga classmates ko at ang iba roon ay mga walang kabulohan na sinasagot naman ni Dazed.

"Sir Dazed may girlfriend ka na ba?" tanong ni Marissa habang nakangiti ng malapad.

Mabilis naman akong binalingan ni Dazed ng tingin kaya naman tinaasan ko ito ng kilay.

"Wala pa, pero malapit na," nakangising saad nito at ako ay kinindatan pa.

In the whole class duration with Dazed ay hindi ako mapakali. Para akong naiihi sa kaba pero hindi naman at angf magaling kong kaibigan ay hindi ako tinantanan.

Sa tuwing magtatama ang mga mata namin ni Dazed ay bigla akong natutulala. His handsome face never fails to make my jaw drop.

"Do you have any questions regarding to our discussion class?" tanong ni Dazed habang nakaupo sa ibabaw ng teacher's table.

He looks hot in his position pero ako ay naiirita dahil maraming nakakaitang iba. It's for my eyes only dapat.

Biglang nagtaas kamay si Lovely na siyang aking kinabigla. "Sir Dazed, I have a question."

"What is it Miss Lovely?"

"Hindi po ba'y engineering student ka? At graduating din. Tanong ko lang po kung bakit naisipan mong sa amin magturo? E, ang layo-layo po ng topics sa criminology and engineering. Ano po ang rason Sir?" tanong ni Lovely habang nakangisi ng malapad.

"Oo nga po Sir!" sigunda naman ng mga classmates ko.

"To be honest with you guys. I am not here to teach, I am here to take a glance at my wifey's gorgeous face," seryosong saad ni Dazed habang nakatitig sa akin.

Panay naman ang pagtili ng aking kaibigan habang paulit-ulit akong tinutulak. Napakagat na lamang ako ng aking pang-oibabang labi at nag-iwas ng tingin. Hindi ko lubos maisip na darating ang araw na ito para sa akin.

"Psst Haven!" sigaw ni Dazed dahilan para mapabaling ang tingin ko rito.

"What?" supladang tanong ko.

"I love you."

Ako ay nagising sa kadahilanang hindi na ako makahinga. Habol hininga akong napabangon at tiningnan ang mukha ng aking asawang hanggang ngayon ay mahimbing pa rin na natutulog.

Buong puwersa ko itong itinulak dahilan para ito ay malaglag sa sahig. Rinig ko ang malakas nitong pagdaing dahilan para ako ay mapangisi.

"What's that for wifey?" nakabusangot nitong tanong habang sapo-sapo ang bewang.

"What's that for ka riyan! Halos mamatay lang naman kasi ako sa sobrang higpit ng pagkakayakap mo," masungit kong saad at inirapan ito.

"My hugs can't kill wifey okay?" nakapamewang nitong sabi.

"It can kill! You—It almost killed me!" singhal ko.

Napabuntong hining na lamang ito at walang pasubaling hinagkan ang labi ko na siyang mabilis ko namang tinugon.

"Good morning Mrs. Scott," nakangiting pagbati sa akin ng aking asawang si Dazed.

"Good morning too Mr. Scott," bati ko pabalik. "Ano pang inaantay mo? Ipagluto mo na ako." utos ko rito na agad naman nitong sinunod.

After I graduated college, Dazed and I got married. We've been in a relationship for almost two years at hindi na nga iyon pinatagal pa ng aking asawa at pinakasalan na ako.

Noong una akala ko'y hindi magwo-work ang sa amin ni Dazed pero ako ay nagkamali. Look at us now, we're both happy and contended. We've been married for six years.

Dazed and I are both busy in our works pero kahit ganon ay hindi pa rin kami nawawalan ng quality time which is needed because we're husband and wife. Dazed is a well-known engineer and I am a police officer kaya naman hindi pa kami nagkakaroon ng supling nang dahil sa trabaho ko.

Every weekend, Dazed and I, goes shopping and date. At sa loob ng weekend na iyon ay parang linta kung kumapit sa akin ang asawa ko. Daig niya pa ang babae sa pagiging clingy at cheesy.

Pero kagaya ng normal na relasyon, nagkakaroon din kami ng problema at pag-aaway ni Dazed na muntik na ring mahantong sa hiwalayan pero nagagawan namin ng paraan. We both reflect after each fight that we have. We both admit our mistakes and apologize.

Ang kailangan sa isang relasyon ay tiwala. Kung wala kang tiwala sa partner mo ay wala iyong patutungohan kundi puro panghihinala at pasakit lamang.

Dazed, whole family accepted me wholeheartedly na siyang hindi ko inaasahan sapagkat nanggaling ako sa isang magulong pamilya. They made me feel the love that I've been longing for so long. Hindi nila ako hinusgahan nang dahil sa pagkatao at istado ko sa buhay kagay rin ng anak nila na siyang asawa ko na ngayon.

"Wifey! Breakfast is ready!" sigaw ni Dazed mula sa kusina kaya naman mabilis akong nagtungo roon.

Isang malapad na ngiti ang gumuhit sa aking labi ng ito ay aking makita. Dazed is wearing a baby pink apron with bear design in the middle. He looks masculine even though what he's wearing is for girls.

"Mukhang masarap ah?" saad ko at malambing na niyakap ito sa likod.

I feel Dazed stiffened because of it making me chuckles. Ganitong-ganito rin kasi ang reaksyon nito no'ng ito ay unang beses na niyakap ko. Mabilis ko itong pinakawalan at naupo sa mahoganing upuan.

Magana akong kumakain ng almusal habang panakanakang tinitingnan ang aking asawang hindi pa rin gumagalaw.

Dazed reactions never fails to amuse me. Kahit matagal na kaming kasal ay ganon pa rin ang epekto nito sa akin at ganon din sa kaniya. Maraming taon na ang nakakaraan pero wala pa ring nagbabago sa aking nararamdaman.

Si Dazed Scott pa rin ang lalaking aking iniibig magmula noon hanggang ngayon. Kahit matagal na kaming kasal ay hindi pa rin ako makapaniwala.

"Dazed, breathe..." saad ko na siyang nagpabalik ng ulirat nito.

Mabilis naman itong naupo at taimtim akong tinitigan. Masuyo ko itong nginitian at kinindatan dahilan para mahina itong mapaubo.

"Are you okay?" kunwari'y nag-aalalang tanong ko.

"Stop doing that!" Dazed exclaimed while pointing the fork in my face.

"Stop doing what?" maang kong tanong.

"Winking! It's killing me!" sigaw nito dahilan para mapatawa ako ng malakas.

"Ang over acting mo naman hubby," komento ko.

Inirapan lamang ako nito at nagpatuloy na sa pagkain. Naiiling ko itong pinagmamasdan habang mahinang tumatawa.

My husband is adorable and hot at the same time kaya nga maraming nagkakagusto rito noon hanggang ngayon na siyang kinaiinis ko. Kulang na lamang ay lagyan ko ito ng karatola na may sulat na 'already married, not available'.

"Psst!" sitsit ko.

Nag-angat naman ito ng tingin at taas kilay akong tiningnan. "What?"

"I love you," seryosong saad ko.

Hindi nakatakas sa aking paningin ang pamumula ng magkabilaang tainga at leeg nito. Mukhang kinilig na naman ang asawa ko.

"Where's my I love you too?" masungit na saad ko dahilan para mariin na mapalunok ito.

"I love you too Haven, so much." seryoso nitong saad habang diretsong nakatingin sa mga mata ko. "Sa bawat araw na ginawa ng Diyos ay mas minamahal lamang kita ng lubos. Sa lahat ng magagandang bagay na dumating sa buhay ko, sayo lamang ako nabuo, nakontento at sumaya ng ganito. Kung may nakakarinig man sa 'kin ngayon paniradong tatawagin akong bakla pero wala e, ito talaga ako pagdating sa 'yo. They often says that she fell first but he fell harder, but in my case, I fell at first sight and I also fell harder every time."

"I love you so much, Dazed. Mahal na mahal kita higit pa sa inaakala mo."

Poems by
Maria Cristina Gornez

Coffee and Treats

I yawn and frown,
While looking at the lawn.
Night lights and busy streets,
Oh, I wish someone will give
me some treats.

So, I went to a coffee shop,
Buying myself a nice cup.
And as I drink from it and
savor its aroma,
I saw a familiar face with a
wonderful aura.

He is in front and staring at me,
Good Lord, I want to flee.
I am nervous and confused,
But why he seems so amused?

I felt giddy and my fingers start to wriggle,
Even my toes start to wiggle.
Now my inside seems revolting,

But somehow, it's a funny feeling.

My world then suddenly stops.
When the rain starts to drop.
The world belongs to us,
And only for us.

But the spell got broken,
When the music starts to play.
A song for the broken,
And those who've been played.

He left and passed me by,
Without even saying goodbye.
And for just a glimpse, I turn around to see,
Just to catch him looking at me.

Until the next time we meet,
Guided by the red thread of fate.
Our cupids then owe us not just a coffee,
But a well deserve loving treat.

Brownies and Brown Eyes

As the sun goes down,
I packed my things and went down.
A tiring day of work,
Now I need a nice perk.

I saw a pastry shop,
And so, I decided to stop.
I choose a newly baked pancake,
And partner it with a milkshake.

Then I sit to eat,
And the taste makes me complete.
Then I heard a beat,
And I began tapping my feet.

I enjoy this feeling,
Free though fleeting.
I can't stop smiling but it's time for me to leave.
So, I drop a tip before I leave.

I walk while staring up at the sky,
Oh, I wish I could fly.
But suddenly I bump into a kid,
I said, "I'm sorry for what I did."

I help him pick up his brownies,
When a man came rushing in worries.
Oh, what a surprise!
This man and his beautiful brown eyes.

He keeps on saying something,
But I'm too focused on other things.
A slight glimpse on his finger,
And there's no sight of promise to forever.

The sight of him reminds me of what I'm missing,
A wonderful and pleasant feeling.
They said it makes the world goes round,
Maybe that's what they call love.

Short Story by
Bhon Glory Jayn P. Cabilete

Revolutionary Ardor

Breaking News: URScout has set a new benchmark beating their previous record...

I am completing the final lines of my poetry collection under, "Welcome to the Revolutionary Ardor", on my laptop. I was excited to see about this boy band's latest professional milestone, and I feel encouraged to keep writing poems.

As soon as my mom saw the screen mentioning URScout, she immediately turned off the television. My mind was thrown into disarray.

I paused typing on the keyboard and looked up in her direction. "M-Mom, why did you turn it off?" I wrinkled my brow, questioning her intention.

She let out a long sigh before turning her face toward me with a bored expression on her face. She even rolled her eyes. "URScout is a bad influence on your future, honey," she chuckled, sneering at me—lifting up her hands to make gestures.

She went on to add, "Look at you, what future will you have by just writing poems and fangirling towards these people who don't even know you?"

My parents encouraged me to pursue a higher-paying course, but I wanted to study literature. I glanced down and ignored my mom. I saw her leave the living room with heavy footsteps.

"Should I regret taking this course? No?" I pondered at the back of my head. "Should I start selling my URScout albums and merch and forget about them? No?" I can't stop thinking about it...

Suddenly, my phone vibrated. One of my online poems recently attracted the attention of a new reader, who left a remark. Even though he does not have a profile picture, I could tell he was a man since his name was Cree.

"Thank you for your poems," he commented, leaving me stunned. The feedback was the shortest I've ever seen in one of my books. In any case, just reading these little expressions of gratitude makes me happy.

Through poetry, I could afford buying URScout albums and merch on my own—but my parents are not happy about it, especially my mom.

I looked around to confirm that no one would be coming. And so, I got up from squatting on the floor carpet to reach out for the remote control. I turned back on the television and switched it to Youtube. I looked for the audio random playlist of URScout' album.

Coincidentally, the first song being played was my favorite feeling. The first two lines appeared on the screen, and I almost swallowed my saliva after being struck by it.

The thought of keeping on penning the poetry made my hands tremble. When the second stanza began appearing next, it struck me right in the feels.

I can't hear the melody, but the words themselves are like singing to my ears.

I can't believe that someone who doesn't know me would make me feel and understand me better. After the song ended, I continued writing.

Your music speaks my voice.

All of our relatives knew that I am a Rescue , and they treated me with the same disdain as anybody else who isn't immersed in the Kpop subculture. Everytime Cree made another comment on my update out of the blue, and with an additional Magenta heart appended at this time, I felt relieved and comforted from all of this hatred.

"You are expressive *insert Magenta heart*." Magenta is the color that represents the URScout Rescues , so, I can't stop wondering if he is a Rescues too.

Is he? For some reason, I wanted to figure it out. It's exciting to meet people with the same taste as yours.

He has given me comments and five stars on every update to my poetry book since this day. Our shared interest led us to WhatsApp, where we exchanged brief messages. It lifted my spirits. He reminds me of URScout.

ONE day, I became part of the top seller poets in the world. I received international recognition and was asked to participate in many high-profile interviews. My first poetry collection book has spawned a series of sequels. I've invested much in real estate and launched a publishing company that seeks poets of today.

Over the years, I have seen Cree's unwavering dedication to my book at every turn. The most surprising thing was that he still sends me an identical message he dropped three years ago.

A constant, "Thank you for your poems or poetry," and sometimes Magenta heart emojis were all the things I could see. I always reply to him back with a Magenta emoji too.

TIME has come, I am finally going to graduate. Following the completion of my last semester of college, I put my savings toward a ticket to see URScout on their world tour. It's 2025, and these guys were making a tremendous return, and I couldn't wait to witness it.

Moments before I was about to go, my mother stepped in and argued, "I can't believe you are still investing in those people who don't even care about you. They still can't feed you when you are hungry." Damn, I know she would still argue about this to me.

But, if we follow her reasoning, then I have no business selling my poetry to those people either, as I have no idea who they are?

However, songs are poems too—with a touch of music. Songs are literature, like mine...

I clarified to her that I would be attending a conference in New York after attending a URScout concert. However, she paid no attention and instead claimed that I was only making excuses. After our dispute, I found myself missing Cree's presence in my most recent poetry collections.

His name isn't anywhere. I'm concerned that maybe he stopped reading my poems. I felt stupid when I realized I was still looking for his name in the comments while traveling. On the aircraft, I exhaled with forced delight; he hadn't even dropped a Magenta heart—even on WhatsApp.

Eventually, I found myself staring at the clouds, hoping that someday I might see him in person.

IT was the day of the concert. My purchase of a royalty ticket gave me access to features not available to others holding standard tickets. Since, with the artists' permission, this hi-touch activity allowed us to meet with them. I couldn't contain my excitement anymore!

Good thing I met a friend, Catie, who works with the deaf community; she was my constant companion and advisor for the time being.

While the other members were entertaining the other Rescues, my heart almost stopped when my bias, Seven Callum, walked towards me. Seeing him in person for the first time is still hard for me to believe. His stare made me feel off-balance. The familiarity in his eyes seemed to convey that we had known one other for a quite long time. He hurried up to me with a broad smile on his face, showing his dimples.

Despite my inability to make out his words, I recognized the shape of his lips and felt like I picked up on at least part of what he was saying. Catie undoubtedly informed him that I am deaf.

After that, Catie asked me to show Callum the diploma I had brought in. Too much time passed before he finally signed it, and it seemed like he was reading it for reasons I couldn't decipher.

Then, just out of the blue, he started doing sign language which completely threw me off guard. Whoa, I had no idea he knew how to communicate to a deaf!

"I am proud of you," he uttered.

I can feel my eyes starting to wet. "Thank you! You are my inspiration to keep going," I replied.

Callum let out a hearty laugh. "I hope we can find a way to spend more time together eventually. I want to play with you and laugh with you more. In the near future... " he unexpectedly added. Catie grasped the meaning of his hand motions. I saw that she was smiling teasingly at me while delivering a subtle squeeze to the side of my waist.

In the end, Callum signaled, "Maxentia," and squeezed my cheeks.

After that, he embraced me tightly out of nowhere. I froze as he taped the back of my head and rubbed it softly. His touch was like an electric shock to my nerve endings.

THE audience enjoyed Gael's opening performance, which included the group's signature brand of awesome dancing movements. They began to sing, but I could not make out a single note. Seeing them perform live brought out the emotion in me along with the rest of the audience. Some of the lyrics that URScout had begun singing are interpreted by Catie.

My heart's rhythmic thumping can be felt all the way from my gut to my brain. As soon as it entered my consciousness and felt the vibrations from the beat, it felt like I understood every word. I felt every tune creeping up my pores. I was able to get the gist of the song from the rhythm of the beats and the way they resonated with my sense of touch.

Their music truly transcends all barriers even for someone like me, who is deaf. These Callum boys from South Reverie, is a work of art.

Later on, Callum's solo performance appeared. He sang a love song. I glanced up at the massive screen as lyrics flew through. Inadvertently, his gaze landed on mine. He saw me in the midst of the Rescues and came up to me unexpectedly.

"I sailed deep oceans to find myself,

But I accidentally got drowned by your tides."

I turned to check whether he was focusing on someone else, but he was staring at me the whole time. I checked the Rescues at my side if they had caught him, but it appeared nobody had noticed.

"You introduced me to this new island—

An undiscovered place of love; no one knows it existed."

I looked away. I can feel my cheek blushing and burning.

My feet refused to leave the venue after the concert. I stared at Callum even after he turned away. When he accidentally looked back at me, I dodged his gaze and hid behind Catie. When he exited the stage, I grabbed Catie's wrist and rushed out of the stadium before he could catch up with us.

"THANK you for your support," I made a gesture towards them, during the time that my readers were waiting in line for a book signing of my poetry collection. I brought Catie with me as my sign language interpreter too for my readers and I to communicate better. They also took pictures with me too.

Their smiles were the result of my hard work for years; it's worth it.

Days after the concert, I flew to New York to attend the book signing and meet my readers. I felt like floating in the air while still thinking about what had happened between me and Seven Callum.

Time flies too fast; it felt like the concert just happened a few seconds ago.

I'm at this formal occasion with a bunch of famous writers, each with their own area of expertise, and I don't feel the slightest bit star-struck. My thoughts kept wandering back to Callum, and it was extremely difficult for me to focus.

Catie returned with some paper a little later. I became puzzled, so I questioned her about it. She replied that a particular someone had given it to her. I cracked it open out of my curiosity and was floored by what I read.

"Thank you for your poems." —Cree

I startled everyone when I suddenly stood up. After asking Catie who provided her this paper, she gave me instructions. She smiles sweetly despite my twitches. She seemed to know this person. Hm...

Soon after I stepped out onto the terrace, I saw a man standing out in the distance. Only his back was visible to me, but he seemed to be someone I had seen before.

C-Callum?

As a response of my disbelief, my pupils widened. When I moved closer to check whether I was seeing the correct person I thought I was, it turned out to be him, Seven Callum.

The moment he turned his back on me, our gazes immediately connected in an instant. I didn't blink even once. He was just standing there, wearing an outfit that fits the dress code of our event. He let out a gasp, and beamed at me with an excited smile on his face.

He knows I am here?!

He gestured out, "Nice to see you again, *Celine*." After stating my pen name at the end, he bowed at the halfway point. My thoughts fell completely silent as my jaw dropped. After all these years, was it indeed him the whole time?!

"You are Cree?"

He nodded before he tapped my head.

He noticed my disbelief and chuckled as he pinched my cheeks once again. Incredulous by what was occurring, he asked me if I was free for dinner. I lowered my gaze and tried to avoid making eye contact with him.

Who am I to say no?

"Are you sure about this?" I asked him.

He quickly replied, "I am always sure about you."

Soon after the event, I found myself sitting in front of him. Even though people were staring at us while we gestured, we enjoyed discussing literature and art.

He expressed, "Thank you for writing those poems."

"Thank you for your music," I replied back. We smiled at one another and exchanged romantic sights. It was the first time I had ever been aware of how loud my heart beats.

He stood, leaned forward and kissed my forehead. —

IT'S 2026. The group had made their next comeback. After he asked me to dinner after their world tour had wrapped up, thereafter it was as if it had never happened. I still remember the unique sensation of his hand on mine. And it felt like his presence had been imprinted on me like a fingerprint up to this point.

He had to catch a flight back to South Reverie so that the group could keep working on their album and music marketing. Hashtags like #RescuesXURScoutUNITED and #WelcomeBackURScout had been scattered all over social media, especially on Twitter. I also joined the trend using my fansite account.

There has been a worldwide upsurge in charity work, and I've been a part of a few of them. After serving South Reverie for three years, Rescues have returned to find that their workload has quadrupled in size. As a poet, I was able to begin the process of rediscovering who I was and reviving my inner life by associating with others who shared the same interest as mine.

"We are Maxentiae!" shouted by my co-Rescues. Their tabloids revealed everything to me about what they were saying.

Thanks to Catie. She stayed with me, interpreting sounds I couldn't hear. My meager popularity as a poet had increased, and now I had security guards watching out for me. By sheer happenstance, a few people recognized me and approached to ask for an autograph on the publications they were carrying.

Our maxentia is URScout, and we ourselves are living proof of their existence. But in reality, everything seemed to be reversed.

They recently dropped some new songs. It was, of course, beyond something we had anticipated for. Bizarre emotions were evoked by the music, creeping into my nerves. I danced with the crowd, enjoying every second of this art.

It sounded similar to cherries and milk, with caramel lips and delicious devilish wings. And just the two of us, embracing this mystery. The prison of you poisoned us severely. I had no one else worthy of respect, and even though I knew the chalice was corrupted, I still devoured it. Into the back of my throat, the liquor is no one else but you...

MONTHS have passed while I still keep on producing poems, an opportunity came for me to venture out script writing or novel writing for a particular movie. Also, days later, Callum added me on WhatsApp with his personal account, not the Cree one anymore. As soon as I saw his name go up on my screen, I could literally hear my heart racing on top of my lungs.

"It's been a long time. Congratulations on your new venture as a script/novel writer!" He messaged. That congratulatory emoji and purple heart at the end stuck me the most.

"You?"

A smile painted on my face. I quickly replied, "Thank you! How are you?"

"I miss you. I want to see you. Can we video call?"

When I saw his response, my heart almost skipped a beat. I glanced around to see whether anyone had seen me squeal with romantic glee. I was so thrilled that I instantly hit the 'like' emoji to react to him.

My knotted hair is the first thing I untangle, and then I focus on the rest of my face. Instantly after I gave him the emoji, he requested a video call, and I almost choked on my own spit when I saw the green button floating!

To facilitate hand gestures, I positioned my phone in front of me. I had to bite my tongue as his live video started playing, and I quickly fled behind the lens. Callum leaned forward, a puzzled look on his face as he tried to figure out where I had been. He made a motion as if he were seeking for me, and when he found me, he flashed his charming dimples.

In fact, he looked even more dashing when he was baffled! I chuckled at the back of my brain.

"Your face looks like you're teasing me to play with you. You want more?" he teased.

Several times, I blinked my eyes as I felt my face begin to blush. I've got this little URScout character pillow at my side, and I keep burying my face in it and shaking my head to get rid of the amorous anticipation that's giving me the jitters.

A few minutes after we finished talking, my stomach started growling. When I checked the time, I remembered that breakfast time had come and gone. Callum saw my reaction and asked about it. After I told him the truth, he abruptly said he needed to hang up since he was late for an appointment.

Disoriented, I massaged my forehead with my hand. Still, maybe his schedule was as full as mine was, and he had to politely decline my call as well. I continue working on the outline for my first book. Sometime later, I heard my doorbell chime. I didn't recognize the name on the delivery receipt, and the delivery guy said he didn't know who had placed the purchase.

I informed Callum about it, and he responded with a few simple yet profound remarks that left me... speechless.

"Eat, I don't want my girl to be hungry."

Callum started dating me for months. Despite his busy schedule, he always makes time to get in touch with me and come see me. With my extensive travel schedule and worldwide commitments, I always found time for him too. The mere fact of being in his presence would motivate me to give my best.

When Catie is on vacation, he represents Catie. It worries me sometimes that he could be in serious trouble. The reality that he's a global phenomenon worried me. He became complacent with the individuals who speak to me and instead tries to figure out how to convey their words via hand gestures.

I tried to convince him that I should get in touch with Catie instead of going after her, but he was hesitant.

In his defense, he said, "I want to be by your side a bit longer since I know I will be busy after this."

I averted my gaze and tried to cover my face, but he continued tugging at my elbows. The moment we turned around to face each other again, he laughed, "You're so cute!" He gave me a little squeeze on the cheeks.

He often pokes fun at me by pressing his cheeks in a playful way. In a playful addition to that, if we are walking beside a busy street, he makes it a point to press our fingers together. When I was unable to feel his contact for a period of time, he would always find a way to seize my hand and intertwine his fingertips, locking me there like he doesn't want me to let go.

Simply seeing these people gazing at us and even taking photographs of us may give me worry at times, and I can't seem to stop it from happening. I often tell him to keep away from me when we are in public areas for our own privacy and protection, but he is such a stubborn guy!

Until then, I withdrew my hands from his. Because he seemed mystified, he halted his progress and came over to me. People were more interested in my presence once he began making motions.

"Is there a problem?"

"They are taking pictures of us..."

The sight of a worldwide celebrity holding hands with a deaf poet like myself caused the crowd to almost stampede, and he turned around to see what had happened. Instead of complying with my request, he leaned in and gave me a peck of kiss on my lips in a snap, leaving me with eyes widened in surprise.

Flashes from the camera began to occupy our sight, almost making us blind as we entered the building towards his favorite museum. He also told me that there is a library here that I surely love.

I covered my face with my bare hand while Callum was bringing me with him.

UNTIL then, rumors have circulated regarding Callum's apparent romantic relationship with me, and our respective companies have been under pressure to release a statement. If the rumors are true, some Rescues showed support, but I have to face the fact that the vast majority of Rescues harbored animosity towards me. This is what I know, albeit I cannot assure whether they are genuine Rescues. A lot of

Callum fans started offering me love and support, but when they found out I'm deaf, some of them kept spouting hatred and told me that Callum does not deserve someone with a disability.

Now, I always end up weeping in my room by myself. Since our schedules are just so diverse, Callum contacts me every once in a while instead of being physically present. He is in South Reverie at the moment, while I am based in New York City due to my projects.

I wasn't able to hear the sound of my sobs, but one thing was for certain: I had a scorching feeling in the center of my chest, and it seemed as if it was going to burst out.

When my mother came to see me, I pretended as if nothing had occurred since she last saw me. It is no longer acceptable for her to say anything that may be seen as hurtful to me. Because of this, whenever I was sad, I would wipe my eyes and try to force a smile.

While I was seated in front of her at this moment, she gazed at me with tears in her eyes. She started crying and immediately rose up to give me a tight embrace.

I froze. I had never experienced a hug from her; this was the first time she did...

My eyes widened in surprise. She tapped my forehead and buried her tears on my shoulders. She began communicating as soon as she took a step back to notice the tired expression on my face.

"I know what happened. I am sorry for not being by your side. I promise to support you during your ups and downs starting today..."

After staring at her, I couldn't stop the tears from streaming down my cheeks. Because of the things that were causing my mind to become so disorganized, I was at a loss as to what I should do or how I should reply.

"I love you, my daughter," she added, making my knees weak.

IT has come to my attention that Callum has not communicated with me for a number of months, and the fact that this has occurred is making me feel anxious. I was looking at the last message he had sent to me, which was telling me that he needed to speak to me at some point in the future. I was gazing at it. It has been weeks, and he still has not sent anything; I am waiting for him to let me know the precise date.

After looking through all of his social media platforms, I was completely taken aback when I read his bio on his Instagram account.

It says, "A water drop surrounding the desert."

After reading those three sentences, I was struck with an unfamiliar and unsettling sensation. I was curious as to what he's been up to as of late. How was he feeling? What about the other members? My heart had to shoulder a great burden. I have seen him and the other members of the band appear on television, and a lot of activities around here in our town are centered around them.

Wherever I go, I see URScout—I see him.

I HAPPENED to come across him during a fan signing event. As soon as I entered the front door, instantaneously, our gazes locked, and he flashed a smile in my direction—a smile that I had been searching for after what seemed like an eternity. He wasn't even surprised to see me here, which caught me off guard.

He requested one of his colleagues to provide him with a whiteboard as well as a marker. I can't stop feeling thrilled about what he was going to say. But, as soon as he showed me the text written on the board, my lips quickly curved upside down.

Huh? My forehead creased in confusion. As I looked into his eyes, he looked at me differently from the way he looked at me before. It felt as if he was just looking for someone similar to other fans that he had met.

I stepped back, making eye contact with him. Until I realized what he was trying to say.

As soon as our managers recognized the emotions on our faces, they gave us the space to communicate. Right at this moment, we were backstage, allowing his other six members to interact with their respective audiences. After that, Callum provided some further details on the matter.

My heart seemed to break down in pieces after hearing his confession. As the leader of the group, he needs to give up his personal freedom to fall in love in order to sustain his career. Our relationship had affected our images; yes, I also felt this too.

He showed me back the whiteboard, and both of us couldn't stop our tears from showing off even a little.

"Maxentia, R-Rescue..." Rescue? He wasn't calling me by my name anymore... "Maxentia, Seven Callum..."

A huge tear cascades down to my cheeks, and it tastes like magenta.

Even though it was just for a little period of time, I will always cherish those times. We let out a painful smile towards one another. Both of us obviously do not want to let go, but we have to.

We have individual dreams that have not been fulfilled yet.

Callum wiped my tears using his fingertips. And, for the last time, he pinched my cheek...before saying goodbye.

"Someday, I will build my own art gallery, and the first artwork I have is you. Please, wait for me..."

Seven Callum, you will always be my "revolutionary ardor."

Poems by Chantel Ruecille C. Bargamento

Masquerade Ball

The ballroom was full of people as the night grew
Laughter could be heard in the halls
Oh, how the time flew

Take me somewhere quieter

I had my fun
Now it's best if I take my leave
Yet whisking me away would be hard to achieve

People went to the theatre

Yet they were there to admire a false identity
A mask I made for everyone
I was loved by none

From a distance, that's when I saw him

A gentleman standing alone
He was drinking punch peacefully
I wonder what it's like to be unknown

Someone asks me to sing a hymn

I gladly oblige, doing it simply to appease the crowd
As I start to sing, he stares at my direction
I blush from the sudden attention

He was easy on the eyes

A handsome face, blue eyes and dark hair
Out of all the men here
No one else could compare

Seeing such a beauty is a surprise

Maybe I could ask for his name
Once I please everyone
Being famous could be a pain

To think that he smiled when the performance was over

Now I remember why I did this
It's easy to escape from one's memory
When you're the prima donna of the century

It's hard to perform and sing when you lose composure

Why does it feel less intimidating?
Now that a certain man's reaction made such impact
It's a breath of fresh air to know he's not judging

Stranger, who are you?

It's almost like you're calling towards me
Although, no one else could see
How the twinkle in your eyes look so pretty

But I know it would be taboo

You're not a noble, aren't you?
As the queen's diamond, I'm destined to marry
Someone who was prim and wealthy

Didn't they say rules were meant to be broken?

The applause rings in my ears
All of a sudden
I could see you disappear

I wouldn't let my feelings be left unspoken

So, I rush through the sea of gowns and suits
Smiling as I walk past ladies
Trying to get to you

For once in my life, I would not be idle

I'd do whatever it takes
Just give me the chance to speak
I will make you fall in love within a week

Who cares about my survival?

If the masses scorn me, so be it
I will not let you get away a second time
We are separated by design

Nevertheless, it's about time I fought for myself

I've been chained by expectations
Not a single moment of this life was mine
Waiting for a single sign

Now I know fate shows itself

Through a dark blue mask that fits your dashing outfit
The grin on my face tells everyone
That I finally lost it

If you please, give me a moment

Let me tell you about me
Let me hold you as you ask me to sing
For you I would until spring

One day I'll suggest elopement

We won't have to wait long
I promise if you ask to be mine
You'll be my muse through all my songs

I'm glad I came

Ever since my rise to stardom
I've been attending these masquerade balls
The time I had with myself was seldom

Tell me your name

An unassuming man like you must have a good one
Dealing with pretentious bastards
With their brains developing backwards

Would you indulge this young lady?

For once, I want no masks
These so-called friends know that
It would be too much to ask
"And to what do I owe the pleasure, my lady?"

Lullaby

As much as I would like to say I didn't dream about us
Heaven would burn to the ground
Before I scoff in disgust

The truth is that I wanted you rather bad

A sudden feeling that I never had
when I was younger
Made a vow I wouldn't love another

The interest and confusion of slowly burning for a fine lad

I swore that I was head over heels

For a man that defended my honour without a command

Even if at that times he tried to conceal

The fact that he did all that because he wanted to

No one told him what he should do

Like a voyager sailing through the dangerous seas

Like how a melody puts the listener at ease

The ambience you gave was a soothing shade of blue

God, I wish you knew how much I love you
Perhaps in another life we'd see each other again
If we met in a noteworthy way, nothing would be askew

Let's start over, shall we?

These are the writings of a love-sick maiden
If you'll be the death of me, that's how I want to go
Don't you see the beauty of being buried six feet below?

He'd rather leave me be

Since the alternative was never getting peace
Everyone told me I was selfish
Would they still say that if I told them I released

The bird from my cage so that it could be free?

From the beginning I knew

That everything I have would soon slip away

So, it's not surprising when he decided he wouldn't stay

Why wallow in sadness when you could see

That we're better if we were two worlds apart

If somebody asks, tell them that

Nothing would stop me from taking this experience to heart

Love comes in many forms

It just so happens that mine comes with abandonment

Because how would you survive my chaos?

I am the personification of pathos

The rose must need thorns

For wherever I go, beauty comes along
With a rule I made, I had to be untouchable since
People are like vines that make me feel like I don't belong

Yet you held me through the scars

Even if these thorns made your fingers bleed
You managed to comfort me
In my time of need

And that moment we shared was ours

I didn't deserve this softness
Everything was surreal, I couldn't believe it
Maybe at the time I wouldn't admit

My darkness fits with your brilliance

Pride and humility intertwined
What a perfect combination
All evident in one conversation

One would admire your perseverance

It's beautiful, don't you agree?
To be the sharp contrast of a writer
That disappears despite being your devotee

It's hilarious

One of these days Moirai would be cruel with her judgement
She might decree I would live forever as a spectre
With no one else knowing better

Stuck in a position that's precarious

It would be a fitting end of an existence that is already dead
Yet as I take my final breath, I hear something
As I lay down my head

The sweet, silvery sound of your voice rings in my ear

Even in my final moments you are here
You just needed to have the final word, didn't you?
I smile as I remember everything that made this lifetime new

You're already dead, but I feel you near

Seven minutes of my life alongside yours flicker in my eyes
We were destined to meet but never to stay together
Either as friends, enemies or lovers

The lullaby I hear reminds me of a cruel summer

A Modern Romance

It's been so long since I've walked through a castle

Seems like it has been a century ago

Trapped in a time capsule

As the machine transports me to a contemporary time

Here I long for where I used to be

How does a person long for a place she hasn't seen?

Like how a traveller is stuck in between

Two paths, yet choosing one would feel like a crime

Forced to stay in the present

Even when your head is in the clouds

In my dreams I sleep on the moon's gleaming crescent

Let me stay in this bliss

However, reality mocks us with its cruelty

As I fall deeper into this present-day, I find it harder to adjust

When I am subjected to watch my people suffer through corruption and un-just

Oh, how authority is quick to dismiss

A flame sparked from within is set ablaze

For some reason it's a feeling one could not be contained

The calendar marks my numbered days

You stay by my side as I plan the revolution

I wouldn't have it any other way

We would have been glorious if we tried

It's a pity that the fire died

This medieval arc has reached its resolution

As I watch the embers fall
We watch the world burn to the ground
When you know I gave it my all

"Take your bow, you did all you can"

The tears make themselves known
Strong arms and a warm chest held me through the sobs
A phantom ache makes the heart throb

A modern romance began

Maybe it blossomed out of pity
Doesn't really matter
When the two of you are happy

It's rather tragic and beautiful, won't you agree?

Everything is not as it seems
Yet we all act like it's nothing during make-believe
A relationship that didn't make someone have the need to deceive

A terrible misfortune we didn't foresee

I guess nothing is meant to last anyway
Should have seen it coming
You just had to have the final say

Only time would tell what becomes of this novel

Sometimes I wish nothing happened
It would have been better if you never came
Love, after what you did, I have never been the same

Nobody should have us as a role model

Unless torment and spite are what they crave for
As characters on a screen, I should tell you
It feels like I've seen this film before

Not another massacre

I don't think that I would make it out alive
Barely survived the first one
An eclipsed sun

Please don't make me suffer

Especially when I am sure things won't get better
Part of me wishes that I wouldn't
But I know I couldn't

You don't know how tiring it is

To quarrel with you as if the world was ending
It probably already did
Memories of you I couldn't get rid

Trying to figure you out is a puzzling quiz

Like a jigsaw puzzle with a thousand pieces
With a monochrome visage
Trying to decipher the lies from your speeches

Here, the director laughs as he plays classical music

I don't understand
Why I was interested in the first place
Maybe it was partly due to your warm embrace

I really hate being love-sick

But I couldn't complain even if I should
Because it had been an enlightening experience
Especially the bad and good

It may or may not have been bad for my health

The following information exceeds a mountain of wealth:
If I had to be a hundred percent honest, you were
A template for the perfect partner

A saint caught the eye of a sinner

House of Cards

Once again, I'm lying awake
Perhaps that I could convince myself
That it wouldn't be a mistake

To think of you in a romantic sense again

Alright fine, I'm lonely
I admitted it, now are you happy?
If you could leave my brain that would be a small mercy

Whether I like it or not you will remain

Of course, it would be too much for you to leave me behind
I remember that you were the only one
Who could ease my mind

What a tragedy that the tables have turned

My sole wish is that I would be blessed with amnesia
For being plagued by you is a nightmare
Nowadays I might even be a millionaire

Since the lesson was never learned

I still think of you when I know I wouldn't
You're still my muse when I write
Even though I shouldn't

Are you fond of poker like I am?

If we were playing, I would've had a garbage hand
Meanwhile you were graced with a royal flush
Whose face wouldn't blush?

As if you were over-prepared for an exam

Yet I had no clue we were going to take one
That seems to happen in real life
Even when you're gone

Some things just never change, don't they?

When we're older, will you stay the same?
Or will you be a different man
You always had a plan

However, you were never one to display

What you had in mind
For the entire world to see
Yet you might not have been blind

Like how I initially thought that you were

It's more likely you knew
Before the thought crossed my head
Now all that I am able to do is lie on my bed

It simply feels like a blur

Maybe everything would have been fine
If all that happened is that I didn't switch my perspective
We could have still been friends if I didn't want you to be mine

Although there's nothing left that I could say

Especially when the bridges we crossed have been burnt
One took offense, one took damage
No one could navigate through the wreckage

When the authorities had to survey

All the emotional baggage that I carry all alone
They say that the reason
For the property damage was unknown

Of course, the hurricane would be invisible to them

He picked up his bags and left the apartment
The man decided to trash it first
Made sure to leave behind the worst

Perhaps what he did should make me want to condemn

His entire bloodline and children
Yet I couldn't bring myself to do anything
All I was able to do was listen

Let me rest in my house of cards

Yet the structure and unstable foundation collapsed
Sometimes I wonder if I'm actually fragile
Even though my body is rather agile

If this was in the medieval times, I'd be a bard

Singing about whatever I fancied
Running around and making sure that
I would never be married

But in this life, I fell for someone

And when I say that I fell, of course I fell hard
How could someone change everything?
Why did I suddenly wish for a diamond ring?

Yet just as suddenly as you came, you were gone

Those cards I bet on you were a waste
Maybe it would have been alright
If I didn't want a taste

But I wanted it, didn't I?

No one could deny the yearnings of the heart
Even if I should have ignored it
I love you, goddamnit
Do I really need a reason why?

A Visit from Your Ghost

The walls of the cathedral are silent
Illuminated by candlelight
One could sense that a spirit was present

No one knows where it came from

Legends say that he was a figment of one's imagination

Some believe it was something lost through the passage of time

While in the near future, an author shares his story through melancholic rhymes

We could only guess what he has become

For not even the woman who loved him most could give you an answer

Their relationship was never straight forward

A few believe they were lovers

But that was the farthest speculation from the truth

In reality, the man of this tale was nothing more than a handsome face

However, the lady saw something that she has never seen before

Based on how it ended, all that she felt was remorse

If only they could turn back to their youth

Nevertheless, time marches on and doesn't wait for anyone
So, they were forced to grow up and grow apart
Leaving temporary happiness and matters of the heart

Oh, how the ghost wanders

Every single memory lingers in places they've been
If a person was able to turn back the clock
You would see their matching grins

Yet, this author wonders

If all that's left of their history are bed time stories
It would be a waste to see this swept away
None of the characters choose to stay

Through the years, no one would even remember their names

What a shame that I choose not to say a word
But it's a small price to pay for salvation
There's nothing here you haven't heard

Perhaps nowadays I have no desire for fame

Living an honest life would suffice
Truth be told, it would be soothing to be at peace
As if the soul was yearning for release

One of these days everything we had would fade away

But as long as I remember you then
I am most certainly sure that day won't be today
For until now I have so much to say

Let these words create a painting I wish to portray

Since I was never that talented with portraits
Although I am a wordsmith
So, it must be fate

Maybe one day everything would be okay

But love, that won't be today
You must find my words redundant
Because genuinely that is all that I have to say

I just hope that my fellow readers would decide to stay

The words of a ghost should be taken seriously
Since most of the time it shows unrest
Even if they try their best

Even if they're living in the present, they're stuck in yesterday

Most of the damn time they don't even have a say
But still we prevail, doing what we can
Even if no one else could understand

Therefore, I decide to join a rambunctious band

It's better than staying in no man's land
I don't have the time to write everything I wish to say
Running out of time, just like what Lim Manuel Miranda used to say

Even so, I do my best to be strong and stand

I have to live, I deserve to
Even if I don't want to go on anymore
I just tell myself I'm doing it for you

Because why would you wish harm upon me?

Nothing could change what we had
Despite all my harsh words and ridiculous insults

I hope that you know that I'm glad

To be a part of a chapter in your book of life
So, now all I do is raise a toast

It was a pleasure being your holy ghost

Short Story by Golden Rose

Once Upon a Time

Prologue

They said love is the reason why many people believed in fairy tales and ends up getting heartbroken. They admired the impossible romance depicted by those illustrations, where a prince charming comes in our lives in an unexpected way and we'd fall in love at first sight and would end up having a happy ending with them. I must confess I am one of those who believe in such fairy tales, where a prince will come my way, and somehow will fall in love, truly in love. I believe in a once upon a time love story that will have its happy ending. I mean I may not be the fairest one of all like Snow White, a sleeping beauty like Aurora, a maiden with a glass slipper like Cinderella, nor have a hair longer than my height like Rapunzel, but there is one thing that we do have in common and that is, we had a once upon a time type of love story where you met one time and suddenly fall in love and somehow you end up together, forever! Is not at all hopeless. As I can certainly be a witness that it is not impossible, it might go into a bumpy ride but it is not hopeless, since I myself have my own once upon a time story.

***

Mangga?

Matagal narin akong hindi nakabalik dito sa probinsya dahil narin sa ang mahal ng pamasahe, at malayo rin kasi. Limang oras sa bus, lilipat na naman sa jeep at sasakay ng dalawang oras tapos mag-tatrisikad na naman papasok sa kanila Cleo, pinsan ko kay Tita Monica, kapatid ni mama. At tsaka, hindi rin ako pinapayagan nila mama na mag-commute papunta rito ng mag-isa. Ayos na sana yung bakasyon na to dahil sa isa sa mga gusto ko talagang balik-balikan rito ay yung swimming pool nila, may free swimming pool kasi sila rito kaya hassle at stress-free talaga. Kaso may summer class yung pinsan ko kaya ako lang mag-isa ngayon dito sa bahay nila. Although andito naman sina tito at tita, ayoko namang makipag-chikahan sa kanila kasi wala rin naman akong masasabi, I mean I may be an 16-year-old lady, but I'm still a kid kaya sure akong wala ring akong machika kay tita at ayoko ring magpunta sa swimming pool lalo na't ako lang mag-isa. Kaya nagpaalam nalang ako na magpunta sa may playground nila. Hindi ganun kalaki ang barangay nila pero malinis, maaliwalas at tahimik. Kahit maliit lang ito, sagana naman sila sa mga prutas at maraming facilities. Like playground, swimming pool, karaoke club at arcade. Ang gara talaga ng barangay nila rito.

Malapit lang rin naman ang bahay nila at ng playground kaya ito nag-mumuni muni nalang ako dito sa may swing. Sa hindi kalayuan nakakita ako ng malaking puno ng mangga at dahil mahilig ako sa mangga, pinuntahan ko ito. May taling naka-lubid sa puno at balak ko na sanang hawakan ng biglang,

"Ahhh!!!" Napahiyaw ako ng may mahulog mula sa puno.

Tao pala, isang lalaki, nakatutok lang ako sa kaniya habang nagpapagpag siya sa damit niya. Katulad ko na shock rin siya ng nakita niyang nakatunganga lang ako sa kaniya.

"Gusto mo ng..." Tumingin siya sa bitbit niyang sando bag at kumuha ng dalawang mangga na may sanga pa, "mangga?" tanong niya sa akin ng naka ngiti.

"Th...thank you..." Inabot niya naman sa kamay ko ang mangga habang speechless pa ako sa nangyari. Men, I was flustered, eh bat ba kasi sa harapan ko pa siya tumalon.

Pagkatapos niyang ibigay sa akin yung mangga, tumingin uli siya sa akin, mata sa mata, tapos tumalikod na siya at naglakad palayo. Kanina flustered lang ako dahil sa pagtalon niya sa harapan ko pero nung lumapit na siya at inilagay sa kamay ko yung mangga at nagkita ang mga mata namin. Hindi na ko flustered, dumbfounded na. My gosh, ang gwapo niya. Ang tangos ng ilong, may kaputian, naka side fringe ang buhok, naka axe body spray pa at grabi flat chested siya pero may msucle, para siyang si Lee Jong Suk, yung body although maganda rin naman yung face niya, hehe.

"Katie!"

Biglang may tumapik sa likod ko, lumingon ako, si Cleo pala, pinsan ko. Nasa 5'3" ang height, dalawang inch lang ang itinaas ko sa kaniya, short wavy hair, kayumanggi, chubby at mas matanda sa akin ng isang taon.

"Anong ginagawa mo dito?" Tanong niya habang tiningnan kung sino yung lalaking naglalakad sa malayuan na halatang tinititigan ko. "Siya ba nagbigay ng manggang yan sayo?" Tanong niya ulit.

"Huh? Pano mo…"

"Itong puno lang ang may ganiyang klaseng bunga ng mangga sa lahat ng manggahan rito. Tsaka si Zane lang ang may hilig akyatin yang manggahang yan." Explain niya sa akin.

"Zane?" Tanong ko naman sa kaniya.

"Oo, Zane pangalan niya, dyan siya nakatira sa may tindahan." Sagot niya sa'kin.

"Sa may kanto, diyan siya nakatira?" Curios kong tanong.

"Oo, bakit? Crush mo siya no?" Pang-aasar naman niya sakin.

"Crush ka diyan, tara na nga." Nag-blush nako kaya nauna nakong maglakad.

"Yieh… pumapag-ibig na insan ko." Ni lagay niya yung isang braso niya sa balikat ko.

"Tumigil ka na nga dyan." Kinurot ko naman siya sa gilid.

"Aray, mapanakit ano ba yan." Nagtawanan kami.

"Tama nga pala. Cley, punta tayong swimming pool." Excited kong sabi sa kaniya.

"May dalawang daan ka ba?" Blank face niya kong tiningnan.

"Da-dalawang daan? Pa-para san?" Nagulantang naman ako sa tanong niya.

"Para sa swimming pool." Sabi niya habang naka-smile na pang-asar.

"Ano???!" Nanlaki ang mga mata ko sa sinabi niya, "da-dalawang daan para maligo dun?" tiningnan ko siya, "pero diba libre yun, anong nangyari?" Tanong ko ulit.

"Mataas na salaysayin, my friend." Sabi niya lang sa akin.

Nanlumo naman ako kasi yun talaga ang gusto kong balikan, other than the arcade yung swimming pool talaga ang namiss ko. Doon kasi ako unang natutong lumangoy tsaka may slides rin kaya ang saya sana non kung free parin yun hanggang ngayon. Hindi naman sa wala akong pera sadyang ang mahal lang kasi talaga ng dalawang-daan. Ayos sana kung isang araw akong nasa tubig, eh isang oras o gawin na nating sampung oras, hehe. Balak ko pa naman sanang mag-renta ng mermaid tail. May mermaid merch kasi sila rito na pinaparentahan nila.

***

Kinabukasan nasa bahay lang kami ni Cleo, sabado kasi kaya wala siyang pasok. Pagkatapos kong hugasan yung mga pinagkainan namin sa agahan, wala kasi silang katulong kaya nag-volunteer nakong maghugas ng kinainan namin, ay nagpunta na ako sa kwarto namin ni Cleo. Tuwing nagbabakasyon talaga kami, sa kwarto niya ako natutulog.

"Hoi!" Tawag sa'kin ni Cleo. Nakahiga kasi ako sa kama, nanlulumo parin dahil sa gusto ko talaga maligo sa swimming pool at makapag-slide ulit.

"Oi." Malungkot ko namang tugon sa kaniya.

"Anyare sa'yo?" Tanong niya sa akin habang may hinahanap sa cabinet niya.

"Bakit ba kasi ang mahal ng-" Hindi ko na natapos ang sasabihin ko ng biglang pumasok si tita sa kwarto.

"Oh, Katie bat hindi ka pa nakahanda, yan na ba susuotin mo maligo ng swimming pool?" Tanong sa'kin ni tita na naka-pang swimming attire na.

"Po?" Tumayo naman agad ako ng marinig ko ang swimming pool na word.

"Bilisan mo na't magbihis ka na. Maliligo tayo ng pool." Naka smile na tumingin si Cleo sa akin tapos binato sa akin ang swimming trunks niya dahil alam niyang ang tataas ng dalang swimming trunks ko at gusto niyang naka-shorts kaming pareho.

Sa sobrang saya ko niyakap ko ng mahigpit si tita at Cleo, grabi miss na miss ko talaga yung pool nila rito, hindi naman sa walang pool sa amin. Kung mahal ang swimming pool nila rito, times five naman sa amin. Although may trabaho sila mama at papa, hindi naman kami pwedeng maligo ng swimming pool palagi. Once or twice a year lang kami nakakapag-resort, its either sa mga swimming pool kung saan iba ang bayad sa entrance at swimming pool o sa dagat na sobra namang polluted, hay nako, siyudad nga naman.

Hi! Nice to meet…you?

"Ehhhhhh!!!" Grabi yung tili ko ng makarating na kami sa swimming pool. Grabi para akong bata na ngayon lang ulit nakakita ng swimming pool.

Nagbayad na sina tita habang kami naman ni Cleo ay naglatag na sa mga pagkain namin sa cottage.

"Hoi! Kanina ka pa nakangisi dyan ah." Pabirong sabi ni Cleo.

"Oi, thank you talaga ng marami ha." Lumapit ako kay Cleo at niyakap siya.

"Ano ka ba, wala to, ganito rin naman kayo sa akin dati eh. Mas sobra pa nga." Sabi niya naman sa akin.

Sa amin na lumaki si Cleo, magkasama na kami since kindergarten. One-year ang pagitan namin, mula bata pa kami, Cley na ang tawag ko sa kaniya, hindi ko kasi ma-pronounce non ang word na "Cleo" kaya Cley nalang ang tawag ko sa kaniya. Hindi naman sa wala akong respeto sa kaniya, ayaw niya rin kasing mag-ate ako sa kaniya dahil nakasanayan narin niyang hindi ako tumatawag ng ate sa kaniya. Kaya kung minsan kapag tumatawag ako ng ate sa kaniya, magugulat talaga siya at iisiping may hihingin na naman ako sa kaniya.

Nagtrabaho sa ibang bansa ang mga magulang niya noon at ngayon na naka-ipon na at nabayaran narin tung bahay ng lolo't lola namin dito sa probinsya, eh sila na ang pinagmay-ari nito. Bunso sa limang magkakapatid ang mama ni Cleo, habang ang mama ko naman ay ang ika-apat, mag-bestfriend na ang mga magulang namin simula bata kaya nakuha rin ata namin ang closeness nila, haha.

"Kate?" Tawag ni Cleo sa akin.

"Oh bakit?" Sagot ko naman sa kaniya.

"Tara renta tayo ng mermaid tails." Excited niyang sabi.

"Huh, eh… Okay, tara."

Nagtungo kami agad sa Mermaid Merch Club na nag-ngangalang "Mercancía de Sirena", nasa gilid lang sila ng ngayo'y "Piscina del Pueblo" na ibig sabihin ay "Village Pool".

Ganito talaga rito, halos espanyol ang mga pangalan ng mga facilities.

***

Nasa tindahan na kami ng "Mercancía de Sirena", may mga swimming suits, trunks, life jackets, goggles, caps, swimming headphones, at marami pang iba. Nagtungo naman kami agad kung saan ang mga buntot naka-display.

"Woah!!!" Sabay naming sabi ni Cleo, ng makita ang buntot na pareho kay Se-hwa ng Legend of the blue sea, yung buntot ni dyesebel, at ang pinaka-fave kong buntot, kay Ariel.

Pinili ni Cleo yung gold tail na kagaya kay Se-hwa yung sa Legend of the blue sea na sirena, habang ako naman, of course, kay Ariel, color green. Sinukat muna namin ang mga napili naming buntot para malaman kung sakto nga sa amin, buti nalang at tamang size lang.

Nagpunta narin kami sa counter, pagdating namin dun, pinakilala agad ako ni Cleo sa cashier at sa isa pang lalaking nakatalikod sa amin, at dahil nakatalikod siya hindi ko nakita yung mukha niya.

"Oi, kayo pala naka-assign rito? Ah, nga pala, Katie siya nga pala, yun si Zane" turo niya sa naka-talikod na lalaki, "ito naman si Karl, anak ng may-ari nitong tindahan" turo niya sa lalaking nasa counter, "Zane, Karl, siya nga pala si Katie, yung kinikwento kong pinsan kong nagbabakasyon dito." Masayang pakikilala ni Cleo sa akin sa mga kaibigan niya.

"Hi, Katie! Welcome to Mercancía de Sirena, ang nag-iisang tindahan na nagbebenta ng buntot ng sirena." Sabay taas niya sa buntot na rerentahan ni Cleo. Mabait si Karl, at nararamdaman kong may pagtangi yata pinsan ko sa ginoong ito. Teka, anong nangyayari sa'kin bat bigla ang lalim ng tagalog ko.

"Hi! Nice to meet-" biglang lumingon yung isang lalaki at, "you?" nanlaki ang mata ko ng makitang ang Zane pala na ipinakikilala ni Cleo ay ang Zane na nagbigay ng mangga sa akin kahapon. Hindi tumingin si Zane sa direksyon ko kaya hindi niya yata nakitang, it's me. Zane, it's me, it is I, your one and only-

"Mag-pinsan nga kayo, mga sirena hilig niyo eh." Patawang sabi ni Karl.

Napurnada daydream ko dahil nagtawanan sina Karl at Cleo, habang ako nakatulala lang kay Zane. Ano bang nangyayari sa akin, but parang nala-lovestruck ako sa kaniya. Hindi na to maganda, masama na to sa health ko, mentally at emotionally. Ano ba!

"Pak!" Sampal ko sa sarili.

"Ouch." Naka-smile kong sabi at nakahawak na sa shorts ko ng may pang-gigigil.

Tinitigan naman ako ng dalawa, oh my gosh anong nangyari…

"Ayos ka lang ba?" Concerned akong tiningnan ni Cleo, nalingat lang ako sandali kay Cleo, at ng ibalik ko yung tingin ko kay Zane, nakatingin narin pala siya sa akin, at mukha siyang concern. Ahhhhh!

"Pak"

Yes, sinampal ko na naman ang sarili ko.

"Ayos ka lang ba?" hinawakan ni Cleo ang ulo ko, "oh my gash bat ang init mo at ang pula mo na."

Ang ganda ng smile niya tapos ang puti pa ng ngipin niya, five times a day ata to nag-totoothbrush eh, tsaka ang li-… li-lipstick? Ahhh ano ba mag-hulos dili ka kapatid, pero yung smile kasi niya eh, yun yung smile niya sakin kahapon.

Diamond in the rough

"Hoi! Okay ka lang?"

Natauhan ako sa tanong ni Cleo, buti nalang talaga at nandito si Cleo para mabalik ako sa katotohanan.

"Ah, oo naman, haha. Nice to meet you, Zane... Karl" Hindi na ako tumingin pa kay Zane at kay Karl na ako tumingin at nakipag-handshake. Nakatingin pala si Karl sa galawan ko kay Zane, the way na hindi ko siya tiningan at pinawis ako ng matindi kahit naka-electric fan naman sa banda namin, alam niya na ata. Ngumiti si Karl sa'kin na para bang may masamang binabalak. Huwag naman sana! Sumenyas si Karl kay Cleo pero dahil knows ko namang may pagka-quite slow yung pinsan ko sa mga ganitong action scene, eh hindi niya nakuha ang senyas ni Karl.

"Ah, Cleo, my friend," anya ni Karl kay Cleo, sabay hatak nito palayo.

"Ouch" Igham ko na nagpangiti naman kay Zane, parang alam niya atang my like si Cleo kay Karl. Eh, ako kaya... alam kaya niya?

"Saan mo ba ko dadalhin?" Blank na sabi ni Cleo, nagalit ata dahil sa pang-aasar ko.

"May papakita lang ako sayo." Ngiting sabi ni Karl kay Cleo tapos dinala niya na ito sa may accessories station. Habang ako ay naiwan kay Zane.

Habang tahimik lang si Zane na nakatitig sa cash register machine, ako naman ay nakatitig lang rin sa kaniya. After siguro ng mga ilang segundo bigla niya akong tiningnan.

"Ito na ba lahat?" Biglang tanong ni Zane sa akin na siyang gumulat sa'kin.

"Ah, eh oo." Sagot ko naman sa kaniya na halata atang abot tenga na ang ngiti ko dahil nginitian niya rin ako.

"Two-five lahat."

"Two five..." Ngiti kong sabi, "Two-five?!" Nanlaki ang mata ko ng maliwanagan ako sa presyong sabi niya.

"Anong two-five pinagsasabi mo?" Sabi naman ni Karl.

Biglang nagsalita si Karl sa likod ko.

"Anong two-five?" Sabi naman ni Cleo.

"Yan yung nakalagay sa total eh." Blankong sagot ni Zane sa amin.

Dali-daling tiningnan ni Karl yung computer.

"Ano ka ba tol, rerentahan lang nila yung buntot eh." Paliwanag ni Karl kay Zane.

Napatawa nalang kami at halatang nahiya si Zane dahil parang namula siya, hehe cute.

"Pasensya, namali ata yung pag-type ko." Sabi niya sa amin ng biglang may tumawag sa telepono niya at kinailangan niyang lumabas.

"Anong nangyari dun?" Tanong ni Cleo.

Ngumiti lang sa amin si Karl at nagbayad na kami. Pina-una nakong palabasin ni Cleo dahil nga sa sigaw ko about sa two-five kanina na limang daan lang naman sana yung total ng pinabili ko kasama na yung rerentahan kong buntot, eh napurnada yung pag-uusap raw nila kanina. Eh sa may pagka-kupido rin ako kaya hinayaan ko muna.

***

Nasa swimming pool na ako kung saan may mga kasama rin akong naka-mermaid tails. Hindi katagalan nandito narin si Cleo.

"So… Crush mo si Zane?"

"Crush mo si Karl?"

Sabay naming tanong. Nagtawanan na kami at nagkwentuhan. Classmates na sina Karl at Cleo simula nung lumipat siya sa lugar nato. Grade 9 siya ng lumipat sila rito at si Karl ang unang naging close niya sa mga classmates niya. Since, magkalapit lang naman yung bahay nila naging mas malapit pa sila. Kaso nga lang,

"May girlfriend na siya eh." Malungkot na sabi ni Cleo sa'kin.

"Ayos lang yan, ano ka ba. Girlfriend lang naman eh, hindi pa sila kasal kaya may pag-asa pa." Pang-comfort ko sa insan ko. "*Ehem* Si Zane may... girlfriend-" Hindi na ako pinatapos ni Cleo at kinwento niya ang background ni Zane sa akin.

Siya nalang pala ang naiwan sa pamilya nila at dinala dito sa probinsya, last year lang siya napunta dito dahil isa pala sila sa napinsala nung bagyo noon sa kabilang siyudad, dagat ang pagitan ng lugar nila sa amin. Ang papa ni Karl at ang papa ni Zane ay magkapatid, sa hindi inaasahang pangyayari wala na siyang mga magulang. Dahil sa hirap ng buhay nila noon sa siyudad, tumigil siya sa pag-aaral para maka-pagtapos ang mga kapatid niya na sa kasawiang-palad ay wala narin. Pagkatapos nung bagyo, kinuha ng papa ni Karl si Zane. Tumutulong siya dito sa kina-Karl para dagdag kita narin habang naghihintay sa pasukan.

"Buti naman at may plano siyang bumalik ng pag-aaral." Sabi ko kay Cleo.

"Alam mo mabait yang si Zane, tumigil ng pag-aaral para sa mga kapatid, nagtrabaho para makatulong sa magulang tapos ngayon wala rin angal ang magulang ni Karl sa kaniya. Sayang rin daw yan eh, matalino raw yan tsaka kita muna naman ang face diba at figures. Grabi, kahit na minsan ko lang marinig na nagsasalita yan, sa tingin ko mabait talaga siya. Siguro dahil sa mga pinagdaanan niya kaya naging ganyan siya, parating blanko ang mukha, walang kabuhay-buhay." Sabi ni Cleo. "Tsaka, ang sagot sa tanong mong may jowa na ba siya, hindi nga yan nagsasalita eh, paano magkakajowa." Sabay slurp niya sa kaniyang orange juice.

"May pagka-diamond in the rough pala siya. A real gem living a rough life." Buntong hininga kong sabi kay Cleo.

"Mag-kikwentuhan nalang ba kayong dalawa dyan." Sabi ni tita sa amin. Malapit lang kasi yung cottage na nakuha nina tita sa swimming pool namin.

"Maligo na kayo tapos umahon muna at kakain na." Sabi ni tita sa amin at umalis narin.

"Opo!" Sabay na sagot namin ni Cleo.

Lumangoy muna kami ng ilang beses tapos umahon na.

A Little Mermaid

Pagkatapos kong kumain, sinuot ko ulit yung buntot ko at lumangoy uli. Lumalangoy ako ngayon sa 10 feet na swimming pool, malayo-layo ang pool na to sa cottage namin mga limang metro siguro ang layo. Ako palang mag-isa rito kasi kumakain pa si Cleo kaya nauna na ako. Sa di kalayuan may nakita akong nahulog sa pool, hindi ko muna pinansin, baka kasi nagdive lang kaya winalang-bahala ko lang kaso halos limang minuto na siya nasa ilalim at hindi ko parin siya nakikitang umahon. Sa sobrang curious ko, nilangoy ko na siya habang sumisisid ako nakita ko na siya, si... Zane!!! Dali-dali akong sumisid at nung nadukot ko na yung damit niya, umahon na agad kami.

"Zane! Zane?!" Tawag ko kay Zane.

Unti-unting bumuka yung mata niya kaso nawalan uli siya ng malay.

Hindi katagalan non dumating si Cleo at tinawag niya agad si Karl na siyang nagdala kay Zane sa clinic. Umuwi narin kami nina Cleo.

***

"Kumusta na kaya si Zane?" Tanong ko kay Cleo.

Nasa bahay na kami ngayon, nasa sala ako habang nasa kusina naman si Cleo, may hinihiwa.

"Nag-text sa'kin si Karl kanina, okay na naman daw si Zane, nahilo lang daw dahil wala pa pala siyang kain simula pa umaga kaya yun. Buti nga raw eh at nandun ka para sagipin siya." Sabi ni Cleo na halatang may nginunguyang pagkain.

Napangiti naman ako sa sinabi niya dahil sa lahat ng pwedeng makasagip sa kaniya ako pa talaga. Sa datingan ko kanina para akong si Ariel ng the little mermaid, with matching kulay berde kong buntot at, well, hindi naman ganun ka red yung hair ko may pagka-reddish lang siya since slight dusty light copper hair yung kulay ng buhok ko, yes, isa ako sa naglagay ng tag-be-benteng hair color sa buhok ko, masisisi niyo ba ako eh sobrang uso non sa siyudad. Tsaka ito lang yung uso na sinabayan ko no. Tapos siya si Prince Eric na nahulog sa bangka at sinagip ko, although nahulog siya sa pool dahil sa nanghihina pala siya, pero parang ganun narin yun.

Pumunta narin ako sa kusina at nakitang kumakain pala siya ng mangga kaya natahimik.

Kumuha narin ako ng mangga, "san galing tong mangga?" tanong ko habang kumuha na rin ng mangga.

"Dala mo to nung isang araw eh, nakita ko sa ref, ayos pa naman kaya hiniwa ko na kaysa naman-"

"Teka di ba may sanga at dahon pa to?" Hindi ko na pinatapos ang sasabihin ni Cleo at hinanap na agad yung sanga at dahon ng mangga.

"Yung sanga tinapon ko na bago ko nilagay to nung isang araw sa ref. Yung dahon parang-"

"Nooooo" Overacting ko namang tugon sa mga pinagsasabi ni Cleo.

Pwede na sanang souvenir yung sanga, kahit dahon man lang sa first meeting namin ni Zane, why???

"Anong nangyayari sa'yo?" Tanong ni Cleo habang kumakain parin ng mangga.

"Akin na yan!" Kinuha ko na yung mangga at kinain at pumunta na ng sala.

"Damot mo!" Sigaw niya habang papalabas na ako sa kusina, "kala mo isang mangga lang yun" sabi niya at nagpalabas ng isa pang mangga, tama dalawa pala yung binigay ni Zane.

Dalawa yung manggang naka-sabit sa sanga ng ibigay ni Zane sa'kin nung isang araw. Hinayaan ko na siyang mag-balat at hiwain yung isang mangga habang nagmumuni-muni naman ako sa may sala.

"Huwag ka ng masyadong mag-drama dyan, ayos na naman si Zane eh" sigaw ni Cleo mula sa kusina.

"Hindi naman ako nagda-drama eh." Hina kong sabi sa sarili.

"Narinig ko yun!" Sigaw niya ulit.

***

After a week, umuwi na sila Zane and there our love story started, char haha.

"Katie?" tawag ni Zane sa'kin, "Salamat ulit sa pagsagip mo sa'kin nung isang araw ha." Sabi ni Zane sa akin tsaka kumuha ng tubig at damn, umiinom siya sa harapan ko, and creepy as it may seem but every time he gulps, his adams apples looks like it is swimming, and in fairness, his actually talking to me, yiehhhhhhh!

Nasa gym kami ngayon dahil may liga ng basketball at isa si Zane sa mga player ng barangay nila. Halos mawalan na ko ng boses kaka-cheer sa kanila and it was worth it!!! Nanalo sila, ahhhhhh!!!

"Woahhh! Congrats sa lahat!" Bati ni Cleo nang lumapit na ang mga players sa upuan namin para kunin ang bags nila. Nasa front seat kasi kami kumbaga.

Sumabay na kami pauwi kina Karl at Zane, at sa totoo lang parang kaming nag-double date, yiehhhh. Si Karl at si Cleo ay nauna ng maglakad while kami ni Zane ay nahuli.

"Congrats sa laro ha, ang galing mo palang mag-dribble." Patawang sabi ko kay Zane.

"Salamat ulit ha." Sabi uli ni Zane, for I don't know, isang libong thank you na ata niya to eh at hindi dahil nag congrats ako sa kaniya kundi dahil sa pagsagip ko sa kaniya non.

"Kanina ka pa ah!" Biro ko naman sa kaniya.

"Hindi, salamat talaga." He shyly spoke.

"Ayos na yun, kahit sino naman siguro gagawin yun." Sagot ko naman sa kaniya.

"Hindi rin, noon kasi muntik narin akong malunod dahil sa walang gusto tumulong sa'kin. Naghintay lang sila na may sasagip sa akin kaya yun, halos isang oras akong nasa ilalim ng tubig. Buti nalang at may lumangoy non sa direksyon ko at dahil nakabukas ang mga mata niya sa pag-sisid, nakita niya ako sa ilalim, kung hindi dahil sa kaniya, siguro wala na ako ngayon." Kwento niya sa akin.

Wala akong masabi dahil sa mga kinwento niya at pati ako nanlumo dahil sa sinapit niya pero at the same time masaya ako dahil nag-share siya sa akin ng personal info niya.

"Hoi, ayos ka lang?" Tanong ni Zane na naka-ngiti ng malaki.

"Oo, naman. Ang bastos naman pala ng mga tao noon at tiningnan ka lang nila." Sabi ko.

"Ano ka ba, nangyari na yun, haha" tumawa lang si Zane.

Please huwag ka ng ngumiti pa ng sobra puputok na pantog ko sa kilig, papatayin mo ata ako sa kilig eh. Ayokong ilagay sa death certificate ko na ang rason ng pagka-deads ko ay dahil sa sborang kilig, ano ba!

"Pero salamat talaga," ulat uli ni Zane, "my little mermaid." Pagpapatuloy niya.

And ladies and gentlemen, I'm dead. Tumawa lang si Zane na siyang nagpatawa narin sa akin, paano ba kasi nakakahawa rin ang tawa niya eh. Hays, first time naming tumawang magkasama, yiehhhhhh. Can we be like this every day, for the rest of our days?

"Katie? Katie?" May sinabi na pala si Zane, hindi ko lang narinig dahil sa daydream ko.

"Bakit?" Sagot ko naman.

"Ayos ka lang ba talaga?" Concerned na tanong ni Zane, hays ang gwapo niya kapag concerned.

"Oo, naman. Bakit ba?" Sagot ko naman sa kaniya.

"Lagpas na kasi tayo sa bahay niyo eh." Sagot naman ni Zane sa akin.

"Huh?" Dang… lagpas na nga kami, "'bat di mo sinabing lumagpas na pala tayo?" tanong ko sa kaniya.

"Eh… hehe"

Nagtawanan nalang kaming dalawa.

***

I love you!

Nasa isang banquet hall kami ngayon. May chandelier, tapos wine glass pa yung gamit na baso tsaka, wow, may chocolate fountain, luxury! Kumain na kami ni Cleo after nang program, tapos nagpaalam muna siya sa'kin dahil nandito rin yung mga kaibigan niya. Nakaupo lang ako sa mesa namin sa may bintana, hinayaan ko muna si Cleo, nakatingin lang ako sa mga nagsasayawan sa gitna ng bulwagan. Hindi katagalan, pumunta muna ako sa labas upang makalanghap ng sariwang hangin. Suot ang off shoulder, emerald green shiny formal sheath gown with sweetheart neck and corset back design na gawa gamit ang high-quality velvet sequin lace, featuring heavy pleated bottom, finished with a 40" long cathedral train. With a white ankle strap high heel.

Naglakad-lakad lang ako hanggang sa napunta ako sa parang garden ng venue.

A large tree was there standing in the middle with fairy lights. Lumapit ako sa puno at nakitang puno pala ng mangga, tumingin ako sa paligid at doon ko palang namalayan ang napaka-gandang tanawin. Iba't-ibang klase ng bulaklak ang makikita sa paligid at may fountain pa kung saan rinig mo ang daloy ng tubig.

I sat in the swing, letting the wind sway me. Kung hindi sa tunog ng kampanang nagpapahiwatig na uwian na, hindi pa siguro ako lilisan sa harden. As I carried my gown, I was stunned by the presence of a man when he suddenly jumped in front of me, a very handsome young man that is.

He smiled at me and I smiled back. We can hear the music playing inside, then someone played Dandelions by Ruth B. on a piano and a lady's voice is heard singing the song. Under the beautiful stars and the shining moon, he asked me if I wanted to dance, and I said yes. He wrapped his right hand around my waist and held tight to my right hand while I held my gown with my left hand, and we started dancing. Lakas maka-cinderella nito, my goodness. It was so good to be true. We were dancing as if kami lang ang natitirang tao sa mundo. He moved so elegantly; it was so romantic.

As we were dancing, the moon then shone brightly, it was so bright that I could see his side fringe of dark black hair, a diamond-shaped face with a narrow forehead, minimal arch eyebrows, a double eyelid, almond-shaped brown eyes, a straight nose, a strong cheekbone, a narrowed chin, and a natural reddish lip. He was wearing a black tuxedo; I looked at him, eye to eye, our faces came closer and…

"Hoi!!!" Pang-gising ni Cleo sa akin.

Naalimpungatan ako sa hoi ni Cleo.

"Noooo!!! Hindi to totoo! Panaginip lang yun?" Laking dismaya ko ng mapagtanto kong panaginip lang pala ang lahat I know it wasn't true, none of it was!!! I was right! It was so good to be true.

"Si Zane ba?" Tanong ni Cleo.

"Anong si Zane?" Mangiyak-ngiyak kong tanong.

"Yung panaginip mo." She spoke, grinning at me.

Kiniliti ko ng husto si Cleo dahil sa ginawa niya. I was sleeping like a baby and had the most amazing dream tapos gigisingin niya lang ako, ano ba naman yan.

Bumaba narin kami ni Cleo at kumain na. Habang kumakain, of course kinwento ko sa kaniya ang napanaginipan ko.

After naming kumain, naghugas nako ng plato tapos biglang nag-ring ang cellphone ko, nagtext si mama.

"Nak, umuwi ka na sa susunod na linggo ha, magpapa-enroll ka pa." Anya ng text ni mama.

"Okay po ma." Reply ko naman.

Tama nga pala isang linggo nalang ako dito kina Cleo at babalik na ulit ako sa siyudad.

Umalis muna si Cleo dahil may pinagawa si tita sa kaniya, kaya ito naiwan na uli ako sa bahay. As usual, nagpaalam nalang akong magpunta sa playground. Habang naglalakad ako papuntang playground nakita ko uli yung puno, kung saan kami unang nagkita ni Zane. Nakita ko uli yung lubid, naka-tali pala ito sa sanga ng puno sa taas at parang ginagamit ng mga umaakyat bilang hawakan patungo sa taas. Ginamit ko ito at umakyat rin sa puno. Ang ganda pala ng view mula rito. Dahil sa ang sariwa nang hangin sa taas eh nakatulog ako. Nagising nalang ako ng biglang may humila sa buhok ko.

"Aray, ano ba?!" Tumingin ako sa baba at si… Zane?

My gash, para tuloy isang kupido itong puno. Parati kaming nagmemeet rito eh. Hindi rin nagtagal ang saya ko ng tiningnan niya ang lubid sa kamay niya at hinatak uli, dun ko na-realize na nagapus pala ang buhok ko sa tali at aray ha, kapatid like kita pero ang sakit na.

"Katie? Anong nangyari?" Concerned niyang tanong. Yieh concerned.

"Teka lang, aray, nagapus yung buhok ko sa lubid, ahhhhhhhh!" Napasigaw ako ng biglang hilain ni Zane ang lubid na may buhok ko kaya nadala ako.

"Aray, ano ba naman yan. Ang sakit sa anit ha." Sabi ko sa Zane na nakatayo na sa harapan ko.

"Nakita mo pala tung lubid." Sabi niya sakin.

"Oo, nandyan na yan kanina nung dumaan ako rito. Noon ko pa nga yan nakita dyan eh." Sagot ko naman habang nakikipag-away sa buhok ko na nakapulupot parin sa tali.

Hindi ko namalayang lumapit pala si Zane sa akin at kinuha sa kamay ko ang buhok ko at lubid. Pagkalipas ng ilang segundo nakawala narin sa pagka-pulupot yung buhok ko.

Dang, habang ginagawa yun ni Zane nakatingin lang ako sa kaniya. Grabi ngayon lang kami naging ganito ka lapit, halos 2 inches nalang ata ang pagitan namin. Ngayon ko lang rin napagtanto na kamukhang-kamukha niya yung lalaki sa panaginip ko, side fringed dark black hair, narrow forehead and chin, the eyebrows, his eyes, his nose, and his lips. Could it be? Sabi nila, dreams have its meaning. Baka way na to ni universe para sabihing, I'm yours and your mine, let's dance as if we're the last human kind.

"Ayos na." Sabi niya sa'kin tapos umupo na siya sa isa sa mga sanga ng puno.

At nagising na naman ako sa katotohanan na ang layo ko pa sa finishing line. Ang layo pa namin sa isa't-isa para magkaroon ng happy ending.

"Salamat." Yun lang ang salitang nasabi ko. Smiling, simping over him.

"Gusto mo ba ng mangga?" Tanong niya sa'kin.

Ah, mango. Do you know, a mango is a symbol of love in many cultures alongside wealth, fertility and happiness. Yeah, love and happiness, hyssss…

"Zane… I love you."

I hate you

"May sinabi ka ba Katie?" Tanong ni Zane sa akin.

"Wa-wala, haha." Damn, hindi niya naman siguro narinig no, oh my gash.

"Ito oh." Sabay bigay niya ng mangga.

"Th-Thank you." Hinug ko yung mangga ng napaka-higpit, not knowing na namantsahan na pala ang damit ko.

"Katie, yung damit mo!" Sabi ni Zane sa akin.

Tiningnan ko ang damit ko, oh my goodness, namantsahan nga ng mangga. Nilagay ko muna sa baba yung mangga at tinry na kunin ang mantsa ng muntik nakong mahulog sa puno dahil sa na-out of balance ako, buti nalang at nahawakan ni Zane ang right hand ko, kundi nabali na talaga ako kong nahulog man ako.

"Thank you, Zane." Sa sobrang saya ko niyakap ko si Zane, for a second, I could hear his pounding chest, it was beating so fast na halos mabingi nako sa kaka-kabog.

"Ayos ka lang?" Tanong ko kay Zane na halatang na shock sa hug ko, "sorry ha, pero thank you talaga." Okay, hindi ko yun ginawa para lang maka-yakap sa kaniya, it was a thank you hug, you know.

"A-ayos lang." Hindi na tumingin si Zane sa akin at bumaba na siya agad ng manggahan.

Umuwi narin ako, still thinking about what happened.

Kinabukasan, pupunta sana kaming arcade ni Cleo kaso may pinuntahan pa siya at iniwan muna ako sa may playground. Sa di kalayuan nakita ko si Zane, mukhang palakad siya patungo sa direksyon ko, kaso ng makita niya ako bigla siyang lumiko na para bang iniiwasan niya ako.

Ilang araw narin ang nagdaan at ganun parin, kung may bibilhin ako sa tindahan ng tita niya at siya ang tindero ay aalis agad siya at tatawagin si Karl, sa swimming pool naman, iniiwasan niya rin ako.

***

Naglalakad-lakad muna ako at tumambay sa playground, may pinagawa pa kasi si tita kay Cleo pero susunod rin daw siya maya-maya lang. Mula sa kina-uupuan ko, kitang-kita rito ang puno ng mangga. Looking back at the previous events, could it be, may mutual understanding kaya kami? It's just a hypothesis, but could it be were just too naive to ask, if we do like each other. Sa sabado na ang alis ko, ibig sabihin dalawang araw nalang ako dito sa probinsya at hindi ko rin alam kong kailan uli ako babalik since magkokolehiyo na ako. Pero dapat bang ako ang maunang mag-confess, like, how? Paano? Ahhhhhh, Zane nagpunta ako rito para mag-relax hindi mas ma-stress, ano ba!

Habang nagsasalita ako sa sarili ko bigla namang dumating si Karl.

"Oi, Katie." Bati sa'kin ni Karl.

"Oh Karl. Anong ginagawa mo rito?" Tanong ko sa kaniya.

"Ito," Sabay turo niya sa bitbit niyang cartoon, "dadalhin ko sa tindahan ni mama. Nga pala, nakita mo ba si Zane?" Tanong niya sa akin.

"Ilang araw niya na nga akong iniiwasan eh." Sagot ko naman kay Karl.

"Oh, lovers quarrel." Dumating na pala si Cleo, and of course, agad niya kong inasar.

"Andito ka na pala. Tsaka anong lovers quarrel pinagsasabi mo. Bigla niya nalang akong di pinapansin eh, akala ko, okay na kami… grrrr" gigil kong kwento sa kanila.

"Ano bang kinakagalit mo dyan?" Pang-asar ni Cleo.

"Ano ba kasi, gusto ba ako ni Zane o hindi?" Tanong ko na napalakas ata dahil sumenyas sa akin ang dalawa na "shh" daw, "bakit niyo ba ako pinapatahimik, gusto ko lang naman malaman eh, sa tingin niyo, may gusto ba siya sa akin o hindi, aalis na ako sa sabado, pagod nakong mag-assume, hindi ako pwedeng-"

"Aalis ka na?"

Biglang may nagsalita sa likod ko. Familiar yung boses niya… lumingon ako and there he was, "Zane?" Tumingin lang siya sa akin.

Naging awkward ang paligid nung dumating siya.

"Karl tawag ka ng mama mo." Tanging sinabi lang ni Zane at aalis na sana siya ng biglang nagsalita si Karl.

"Ah, tol baka may gusto kang sabihin kay Katie." Sumenyas agad siya kay Zane.

"Oo nga Zane." Pagsang-ayon naman ni Cleo.

"Umph, ingat sa byahe." Tanging nasabi lang ni Zane at ngumiti sa'kin.

What? Yun na yun? After niya marinig ang lahat? Anong nangyayari?

"Teka, Zane?" Sigaw ko kay Zane, "wala ka na ba talagang ibang sasabihin sa akin?"

Please, confess, if gusto mo ko sabihin mo na, maawa ka naman.

"Karl…" tumingin si Cleo kay Karl at sumenyas na umalis na sila, na siyang ginawa naman ni Karl. Pero ang totoo nasa bandang slide lang sila, labing-pitong hakbang mula sa amin.

"Wala ka ba talagang sasabihin sa akin?" Tanong ko ulit kay Zane.

"Ingat sa byahe mo." Sabi niya, nihindi man lang niya ko tiningnan.

"Sa sabado pa naman ang lakad ko eh, kung dahil to sa hug, I'm sorry."

"Hindi, ayos lang, kung sa tingin mo dahil to dun, hindi, may ginagawa lang talaga ako, kaya nagmamadali ako. Pinahanap lang ni tita-"

"Yung totoo… gusto mo rin ba-"

"May girlfriend na ako."

Hindi man lang siya kumurap, mata sa mata, sinabi niyang may girlfriend na siya.

"I hate you."

The end?

"I hate you" ulat ko sa sarili, "pwede paki ulit?" tanong ko sa kaniya.

Bumuntong-hininga muna siya at, "may girlfriend na ako Kate." saad niya.

"Ta-talaga? Wow, congrats! Salamat, at... umph... *ehem* nalaman ko ng, masaya ka na pala, haha" isang hakbang palayo, unti-unti akong lumayo sa kaniya, gusto ko ng umiyak pero pinigilan ko ang sarili ko, this is why assumption is a bad habit. Tumalikod na ako at aalis na sana ng hawakan niya ang kamay ko na siyang nagpahinto sa akin.

"Anong ginagawa mo?" Tanong ko sa kaniya without looking at him.

"I'm sorry," binitawan niya na ang kamay ko.

"Ba't ka ba nagso-sorry wala ka namang kasalanan, haha. Congrats uli, sana maging masaya kayo." Sabi ko at tumakbo na.

It was so embarrassing, ano ba kasing iniisip ko. That he would like me, what a joke!

Overacting man kung sabihin but I cried my heart out because of him, he was not worth it for my tears, but he had my heart and it devastates me.

***

Dumating narin ang araw na aalis na'ko ng probinsya, and yes hindi na kami uli nagkita pa ni Zane after non. I came here, hoping to relax but then I met him, I was a kid who thought I finally found my prince, unfortunately he was already someone else's prince. I hope maging masaya sila, brokenhearted man at least I did fall in love, it's just, unfortunately, walang happy ending.

I went back to the city, heartbroken. I hated myself for not able to date a guy when I was in college as my heart was still with him. He was, he was my first love, my first heartache. The person I thought was my prince charming, he was supposed to be my happy ending, or so I thought.

A whole decade has passed after our encounter, it was truly a once upon a time, as it only happened to me once. I never felt the same way again to anyone. While in college, I got an admission here in States and took the opportunity. Cleo is now a mother of two beautiful kids, she moved in with me before getting married, here in States. She met her husband in the workplace, he wasn't no Karl, but she fell in love the same way she fell for Karl. Only this time, he took the hint and they got married.

I, on the other hand, spent most of my time teaching and tutoring. I wasn't in a hurry in getting married, so I took the slow pace.

Everything in my life went okay, until I met Karl again.

***

I was sitting alone in a café, waiting for my drink when a familiar voice, talked to me.

"Katie?" The man asked.

That voice, seemed so familiar. I looked back and saw;

"Karl?" I gasped seeing him.

"Kumusta!" Sabay naming tanong sa isa't-isa.

"Have a seat. Kumusta ka na?" I asked.

"Ito, ganun parin. Ikaw ang kumusta, hindi na uli kita nakita sa probinsya ah." He spoke.

"Ah, oo, nagka-scholarship ako rito eh, kaya kinuha ko na." Sabi ko.

"Eh, si… Cleo. Kumusta na siya. After college, hindi ko na rin siya nakita eh." Saad niya.

"Ah oo, sumama siya sa akin rito." I happily responded, dumating narin yung waiter at binigay ang kape ko, "maayos naman na siya." I continued.

"Mabuti naman kung ganun." Sagot niya.

"Ayon may asawa't anak na." I continued, which made Karl's smile fade away.

"Talaga?" Tanong naman niya.

"Hindi mo ba alam?" I asked back.

"Hindi eh, ngayon lang rin kasi ako nakababa ng barko, isa na kasi akong seaman ngayon." He explained.

"I'm happy to hear that, sana maging masaya ka narin." I said to a sad Karl.

We were still talking when he got a phone call, he said he needed to go and said our goodbyes.

Habang naglalakad ako pauwi, tumambay muna ako sa may park kung saan may puno ng mangga rin. Katulad nun sa probinsya, malaki rin ang puno dito. Looking at the tree, si Zane ang parati kong naiisipan. Kumusta na kaya siya, I had the urge to ask Karl about him kaso naunahan ako ng kaba and was not able to. Besides, what was I gonna ask, kumusta na si Zane, may asawa na ba siya, nagka-happy ending ba sila ng jowa niya non? I've got so many questions I wanted to ask, but Zane was the only one who can answer them.

What he did was really heartbreaking for me, but I can't just blame him. Hindi niya rin naman kasi sinabi na "love me", it was I who loved him.

***

Two weeks after, we were scheduled to attend a convention. A teacher's convention, a lot of teachers has gathered today for this particular event. From different countries and grade level.

It was no new thing for me, every year may convention talagang nagaganap, and I must attend every one of them. Ang kaibahan nga lang ng convention na ito ay sa isang banquet hall ang venue at nirequest ng host na maka-formal attire ang mga guest. A request we must do.

I wore an off shoulder, emerald green shiny formal sheath gown with sweetheart neck and corset back design na gawa gamit ang high-quality velvet sequin lace, with a white ankle strap high heel.

After the said convention I went outside to breath some fresh air, dun nakita ko ang isang puno na kaparehas na kaparehas ng puno sa park malapit sa apartment ko. I went there and sat until a guy asked if the seat was taken, I said no and he sat beside me. He was wearing a tuxedo, after a minute or so, tiningnan ko ang nametag niya, it says Mr. Garcia, from Philippines.

"You're from the Philippines?" I asked, politely.

"Yes." He spoke.

I couldn't see his face properly kasi wala masyadong light sa inuupuan namin but that voice seemed so familiar.

"I'm sorry, but do I know you?" I asked.

"Nakalimutan mo na ba talaga ako?" He smirked.

And in that moment, I knew, he was,

"Hi, Katie, it's me-"

"Zane" Sabay naming sabi.

Hindi ko maintindihan ang naramdaman ko non, should I be happy, what should I ask, what should I do?

"Naging guro ka pala?" He asked.

"Yeah."

"Ang dami ng nagbago sayo ah." He shyly spoke.

"Ikaw rin. Mas talkative kana ngayon unlike last time." I said, smiling, remembering our time together.

"Yeah, I've worked on my social skills." He said, joking.

"Good for you."

"I'm sorry."

I just shrugged; I didn't know what he was sorry about.

"Wala talaga akong girlfriend." He said, looking at me.

"Huh?" I froze. Anong pinagsasabi niya?

"I just used it as a silly excuse, sobrang torpe ko lang talaga noon." He said, not looking at me.

"Anong ibig mong sabihin?" I asked curiously.

"I guess it's time for my confession. I guess this is the end."

Confession

"I guess it's time for my confession. I guess this is the end."

"Anong ibig mong sabihin?"

He looked at me and held my hand, "I liked you."

Nanlaki ang mga mata ko ng sabihin niyang… gusto niya ko?

"Simula pa nung una kitang nakita sa labas ng bahay nina Cleo. Nung narinig kong pupunta ka ng plaground, humingi rin ako ng pahintulot para magpunta ng manggahan. Dali-dali akong umakyat non para di mo ko makita, tinantsa ko talaga ang pagtalon ko sa pagdating mo." He smiled. "Kahit ang sakit ng paa ko non dahil sa pagtalon ko, hindi ko pinakita yun sayo. I wanted to look cool in front of you." He looked at me and looked away shyly, continuing his confession. "After I gave you the mango, I was smiling like an idiot walking back home. I couldn't understand what I was feeling at that time. Nung nakita ko kayong papasok non sa may swimming pool, nagpanggap akong may ginagawa at tumalikod sa inyo para kunwari hindi ko alam na ikaw pala yun. Nung ewan tayo nina Cleo at Karl sa may counter, hindi ko mapigilang ngumiti, nasa harapan na kita pero hindi ko masabing gusto kita sa mga panahong yun."

"I wanted to tell you I like you. Especially after you saved me, pero naunahan na ko ng kaba eh, natatakot rin kasi ako baka di mo ko sagutin." He just looked down, letting go of my hand. "I'm sorry kung hindi ako nakapag confess sayo non, it took me so long to tell you this." He finally looked at me.

"Yeah, it did take you long enough-" suddenly my phone rang, "hello?"

"Mommy? Hi, mom, where are you?" The other line asked.

"Hey, sweetie, mommy's still at the convention. Aren't you asleep yet."

"I'm going to, I just called to say good night, love you."

"Love you, love. Sweet dreams." The call ended.

Lumingon ako sa nakatulalang Zane, his expression was the same as to when I hugged him before on the mango tree.

"I'm so sorry, I can't believe I just confessed to a married woman. I'm so sorry, I don't intend to ruin your married life. I'm so-"

"Zane?" I looked at him, holding his hand, "I'm not yet married."

He looked at my finger and saw no wedding ring.

"So sino yung-"

"She's Cleo's daughter, iniwan muna niya sa akin ang pangalawa niya kasi umuwi sila ng pinas to get the oldest who is visiting Tita Monica. She's not mine, and also... I haven't found my happy ending, yet." I told him, making sure that there is nothing to say sorry about.

He held both my hands and "I know this may seem too fast pero I don't want to take any more chances, Katie... will you be my girlfriend?" He asked me as our eyes locked.

Totoo na ba talaga to, hindi na panaginip? I pinched myself before saying "Yes" I answered after knowing, this is reality.

We embraced each other, crying as it took as 10 years to finally be together. Who would think that in a matter of seconds, I would find my happy ending.

"Katie?"

"Hmm?"

"Should we start over again?"

"Start what?"

He took something from his right pocket, "Mangga?"

"Th-Thank you"

"Ako nga pala si Zane." He moved his hand and asked me for a handshake.

I took his hand and, "Nice to meet... you!" I smiled, "The name is Katie" we shake hands. He shake my hands badly, "ah, diamond in the rough, ey?" He smirked, he knows exactly what he was doing, "you lack manners, dear." I pushed his hand from mine.

He wrapped his hands around my waist and pulled me closer to him, "said by a little mermaid?" I looked at him as he was still smirking at me, bullying my height.

"I love you," he continued, while I can only murmur " I hate you."

He leaned closer, our face came so close that I had to jumped out of his embraced,

"Okay, that's it, the end." I walked away from him.

"The end?" He ran towards me, " but we were just starting, I just finished my confession." He hugged me backwards, I turned, looking at him,

"I love you, my prince."

"I love you, my happy ending."

Short Story by
Arius Lauren Raposas

How Would You Unlove Me?

Introduction:

"Hey, what breakup?"

Geine Mark Aurelio found himself in a pinch on the first day of his job, but not because of anything related to his performance. Upon entering the obscure government agency called Bureau of Information Management and Media Operations (BIMMO), a female coworker he barely knew claimed they just broke up. Now, she had the entire office on her side.

Or did he hardly recognize her? Arya Bernice Santoria appeared to hold a lot of evidence backing up the "years they have been together." So, what really happened between them?

This unlikely story took shape in the context of a secret project of utmost national importance, codenamed BIMMO 10314.

First Thing In The Morning

"Starting right and strong. Hello world! Let's go!"

A good day led to a good life. This is what the masked Geine Mark Aurelio, aged 26, held fast in his heart as he walks confidently to his new workplace. After working relatively low-ranking positions in three different government agencies, the bifocaled young man clad in smart casual attire believes it is about time for him to finally make a mark. His new office, the Bureau of Information Management and Media Operations, or BIMMO for short, was generous enough to grant him a middle-ranked position: senior writer. It usually required five years of relevant experience, as well as 80 hours of relevant training, but three years after his college graduation, he built up an impressive resume that led BIMMO to give him a special consideration for the role. All he needs to do is open the glass doors, and this exciting new phase of his life will begin. What else is more thrilling than becoming a fresh cog of the esteemed bureaucratic machinery?

"Still," he thought to himself, "how would I be received there? I've got the experience, but come to think of it, I never really stuck in any one office…"

Dark clouds gathered inside the white-walled office full of cubicles divided by glass panels. All eyes suddenly focus on Aurelio, their gaze enough to melt the insides of a professional coming out of a brief unemployment, as the masked faces would mean revealing their respective temperaments through the eyes. It took a short three months for him to find this new line of service, record time in an economy which suffered rock bottom.

As he tried his best to ignore them, Aurelio could not help but think, "What have I done?! I'm not late, am I?! They're literally killing me!"

His enthusiasm quickly dissipating, there seemed to be light at the end of the tunnel when he saw their calm, smiling supervisor in a white jacket, the 39-year old Rednaxela Dakila.

"S-Sir Dakila," Aurelio stuttered, "w-what's…?"

Dakila put up his gloved left hand, "Please, Geine. Red will be fine, unless you want me to call you Mr. Aurelio?"

"Y-yes, Sir Red…"

"Mm. With that out of the way," Dakila walks him to a cubicle near the conference room, "Would you care to explain what's happening here?"

Aurelio could not believe his eyes. Almost all the girls of the office, which really meant five out of seven, flocking to one of his coworkers, a sobbing young woman donning a blazer and a skirt. Then again, he was more concerned about them being earlier than him than anything else.

The females surrounding her screamed, "There he is! Get him!"

One by one, they lunged against Aurelio with pens, rulers, monopods, even scissors and forks. As if instantly, he was warped into an augmented reality. Health point (HP) bars popped out of their heads like tongues of fire, their bodies became life-sized heat maps which seem to help in predicting motion, and the office supplies they hold translated into *weapons* of potential damage. His visual prowess activated to help him dodge every attack within such a cramped space. With a ruler stuck between his armpit and a pen caught in his hair, Supervisor Dakila looks at their early morning theatrics with dead eyes.

"Girls, please," Dakila finally mustered the courage to speak up, "I believe we need a fair trial."

While his words seemed to fall on deaf ears, the women did stop from their reckless offensive. Instead, they formed a circle, a wall of death if one willed, with their w*eapons* at the ready.

"I dreamed once that a bunch of girls were fighting for me," the shaky Aurelio thought to himself upon realizing his position, "but not to fight against all of them!"

"Stop! What do you think you're doing, wasting precious public resources?!"

A thunderous voice cuts through the gloomy battlefield. They all turned to the office entrance, only to witness the fiery descent of the so-called Dark

Angel. Wearing a black coat and slacks, the 35-year old BIMMO Chief Angela Seo has made her jumpscare entry with her long black hair rising behind her, as if taking flight. Aurelio's video game fantasy steered back to reality. The attention had instantaneously shifted to hail the chief.

She glared at the supervisor, "What's the meaning of this, Red?!"

"Ma'am! Ah, well, you see," were the words that can be heard from Dakila before he whispered the rest of his narrative.

Seo's scary look became a sympathetic one when she has heard everything Dakila had to say.

"Okay, let's hear it then," she looked at Aurelio and the rest of the office staff with folded arms, "We'll use the conference room."

Everyone followed Seo's lead. The conference room also had the white walls like the rest of the office. The glass windows dominated one side of the room, letting one have a wide view of the city. After all, the BIMMO office was located at the 14th floor of a building the government rents from a private tower mall. In reality, it was the 13th floor of the said edifice, only that the superstitious builders decided to skip the counting from 12 to 14. Those who sought to rent the space knew better, however, and nobody wanted to take the space until BIMMO came in. Chief Seo, also being the superstitious person, made modifications to negate the *bad energy* of that floor, and the conference room is the epitome of those measures. Potted plants were placed on the four corners of the room. Four dragon statuettes were put in the center of the oval conference table, each one facing a cardinal direction (that is, north, east, west, and south). The dragon's mouth and head had salt in them, which Seo ordered to be replaced every day. This is the dragon's "daily intake" to replenish its power. Two smaller tables were allotted for telephones, which have a sitting lion beside each. Lastly, the standing air conditioner was installed with wheels in order to have it facing the lucky direction allotted for a certain day. For this day, it faces the southwest direction.

Chief Seo seated at the capital of the conference table. Meanwhile, Supervisor Dakila seated at the other end. The two employees nearest Seo would be Aurelio and the crying female coworker.

"This noble court accepts the case of Geine Mark Aurelio versus Arya Bernice Santoria," Seo declared before tapping the table with her hand.

"M-Ma'am Seo," Aurelio protests, "What's going on? And it's Geine as in Jin, not gain…"

"Whatever," she waved her hand in the air, "Do you deny all charges?"

"W-what charges, ma'am? I-is this an administrative ruling?"

The rest of the coworkers, with the exception of Dakila, booed at Aurelio. They feigned throwing stuff at him, even though they were not holding anything.

Santoria's crying slowly subsided, "Chief, I... You don't... We don't have to do this..."

Seo patted her employee's shoulder, "How courageous of you to still cover up for him, but you're no longer together now."

With much concern, Aurelio stared at Dakila, and then at Seo. Would he be fired without even working for a single day? Worse, would all the requirements he painstakingly fulfilled be all for nothing? What a waste of resources only to be unemployed again!

Then, it hit him. Arya Bernice Santoria? Santoria... Had he not heard of this name before? Santorini, perhaps, but that was the tourist destination at Greece. Think. Think harder.

"You," Santoria removed her mask and pointed a finger at him, "How dare you forget?! We just broke up!"

Aurelio bellowed, quite involuntarily, "Hey, what breakup?!"

She burst to tears once more while searching her bag. It did not take long before she took out what seemed like a photo album. Considering the technological pace, such a bulky album was supposedly no longer in style, but somehow, Santoria had it well kept.

"Men...," Seo muttered to herself.

When Santoria opened the album, the first photo featured her and Aurelio in a winning team of a certain quiz bee. And by team, it meant just three participants. It seemed like an old image, considering the overall quality, hailing from a time before smartphones and high-speed internet.

She traced her finger on the first photo, "Look, here I am, and that's you. Right beside me!"

Unbelief is evident with Aurelio, "That's you?!"

Her appearance then differed from her current look. Today, she had her hair cut short, going down to the shoulders only, and a clip keeping her bangs on one side of her head. She wore almost no makeup, except for lip tint that gave a natural glow to her lips. In the throwback of a photo, she had long hair flowing down to her waist, and makeup was quite evident on her gleaming face. More so, she did not have eyeglasses then. She donned a pair now. Would this be the so-called Superman effect, when wearing glasses made one look a whole new person?

"Surely you've heard of photo editing!" Aurelio appealed, "I haven't seen this girl until now!"

One of the female coworkers coughed, "Denial. The first stage of every breakup."

Meanwhile, Santoria frowned as she flipped the following pages, "Then, how about this?"

It was her selfie with Aurelio. But perhaps taken without his consent. Who could say? The photo showed one side of Aurelio's face as he boards the jeep. This was not the sports vehicle Jeep that traversed all terrains known to humanity. It was the wartime service vehicle converted into a public transport mode after the war with surplus parts. These jeeps were slowly being modernized, making them not appear like the traditional jeeps anymore, but this aging *king of the road* still reigned to this day despite the powerful force of technological progress.

"You said you're going ahead of me first to check if the jeep is good to ride in," she continued, "Look here, it's another photo of us in the bus."

In yet another selfie, Aurelio could be seen sitting with an old woman beside him. Apparently, Santoria was standing in the aisle.

Seo remarked, "How ungentlemanly."

"No, you don't understand," Santoria interjected, "He said the seat was hard to sit on, so instead of letting me endure the uncomfortable bus seat, he took…"

"What a lame excuse," some of the female coworkers protested, "Is chivalry dead?!"

As she showed another photo of them, this time in a train, Aurelio could just gape.

"Wait, you were there?" or so he thought he had said, but no words came out from his mouth.

The cautious person that he was, Aurelio was quite sure to always look and listen at his surroundings. If there were any suspicious activity around him, he would have noticed it already. But here came Santoria. Could he not feel her presence then? Or was she a world-class professional at this? There were so many photographs, he could not even recall what he was doing at some of those moments, but she seemed to know every detail. She was even happily reminiscing with all the nostalgia.

After checking the overwhelming evidence, Seo sternly asked, "Well then, Geine? We don't have all day!"

"M-Miss Santoria…" a defeated Aurelio looked down, "W-why? Why are you doing this?"

What else could be said? In his mind, the thought of being laid off first thing in the morning would probably be the worst-case scenario for a new employee seeking to emerge from the claws of poverty.

"No," an adamant Santoria faced Aurelio, "I'm the one who should be asking that! I've done everything for you to notice my efforts! Why can't you love me back, just as I love you?!"

"Wow, that escalated quickly," Dakila thought to himself.

As the rest of the coworkers voiced their support of Santoria, Aurelio stood, bowed to everybody in the room, and gritted his teeth, "I have nothing else to say. I'm sorry. If I may be excused."

When he left in such haste, Santoria could not help but lovingly gaze at his frame.

"Was I too hard on him?" she pondered, "Get it together, Arya! This is your first step."

Meanwhile, Seo motioned her head, which Dakila acknowledges. The supervisor departed as well, only to find out Aurelio had already left the office. Fortunately for him, he was able to catch their new employee just outside the building.

"Geine, wait up!"

Aurelio was about to board a van when he heard the BIMMO supervisor hailing. He stopped without turning around.

"What is it, Sir Red?"

Dakila puffed for a while before speaking, "You're going home? It's not yet–"

The van driver yelled, "You two! If you're going to hold the line, don't do it here! I've got a business to run! We're only at 50 percent capacity and all!"

They nod, quietly moving away from the terminal to the nearby sidewalk.

"Geine," Dakila then broke the silence, "I know how you feel."

"Sir, before you go any further, let me make this clear," Aurelio calmly looked at him with clenched fists, "I don't care less if I'm judged as that woman's ex, or as a person who has abandoned the principles of a nice guy. What I can't stand is being challenged for my integrity and character."

"So, what will you do now? Personally, we'd really like to have you here. And I believe CAS thinks so, too. Take my word for it."

"CAS?"

"Ma'am Seo."

"I see… It's easy for me to quit, sir. I can draft a resignation letter in seconds. But to be frank, I need this job. I'm the household's breadwinner. I might be worthless in your eyes, but I'm a professional. I have reasons to work my best, sir."

A smile shined in Dakila's face, "A professional, eh? I'll be glad to work with you then, Geine."

The supervisor wrapped an arm around Aurelio's shoulder, and accompanied him back to the office. However, there was one line of thought that revolved in his mind for the rest of the day.

"If you love me, how would you unlove me?"

Top Secret Mission

"Hi, I'm Geine, and there's a lot of things to dislike about me."

He could just blurt that out, because despite Dakila's uplifting introductions for Aurelio the following day, the latter already had more than half the office members prejudiced against him. There would have been 12 members overall, headed by BIMMO Chief Seo. Below her managing the gritty daily affairs was Supervisor Dakila. Besides Aurelio, there were three other writers. Two of the staff handled the administrative tasks, while the remaining four were assigned in the creative department. BIMMO had two illustrators, and two photographers serving also as videographers.

"Team, we'll have a meeting today," Dakila proclaimed, "Luckily, we won't have CAS with us."

"Luckily, sir?" one of the employees asked.

"I meant sadly."

The entire office, save the two administrative staffers who remained working in their posts, took their seats almost immediately. Dakila seated at the capital of the conference table, while Aurelio took a seat at the far end. Evidently, no one wanted to sit beside the man who supposedly *dumped* Santoria on his first day on the job.

"Alright, guys and gals," Dakila began with a single clap, "The older ones here, I know you're fed up with it, but here we are to realign ourselves to the top secret mission we are doing."

Aurelio raised his eyebrows, but when he saw he was the only one with such a reaction, he immediately took an uninterested look to conform.

The room dimmed and a large LED screen has revealed itself from a revolving part of the wall. It turned out to be a video which gave a warning written in bloody red: For Your Eyes Only. Then, a song boomed from the video, as if it were an opening theme of a movie or series. Along with it were animations of certain periods in history produced by different animators mixed together so much, they did not seem to be synchronized and fitting for each other at all. Soon, the song faded as a figure emerged from dark smoke erasing the entire background.

The figure turned out to be Seo herself, who proceeded with a scripted narration, "Welcome to BIMMO 10314, the top secret project that will save this country! Let's get down to business!"

Dakila could only sigh. Either because he had seen the video multiple times, or because of the video quality. Perhaps both. Meanwhile, the intro left Aurelio wide-eyed. There were so many elements mashed together without much sense, but somehow, it did catch one's attention.

"As you can see," Seo continued, this time carrying a metal stick while having charts and graphs in an office setting behind her, "nationalism and patriotism is the blood of every country. If the nation is an imagined community, it is the imagination that keeps us together."

She then described how nationalism was on the rise in a global scale, but nationalism in the local scale has significantly decreased, especially among the youth. While scholars have argued that averages, as demonstrated by numerous surveys, could not be seen as a worldwide trend, the same set of surveys show that the nation's citizens in particular suffered a huge drop in possessing national pride and affinity. They were better off called as Americans, Europeans, Japanese, Koreans, but never as their own nationality, even when inside their own country. Love of country, what else should be more supreme? As far as the data goes, a lot would be regarded higher.

"Therefore," Seo tapped the stick strongly on the charts, "I've come up with..."

The BIMMO chief narrowed her eyes, so much so that they appear like thin lines on the screen.

"I mean, yes, we. It's we... We've come up with a surefire way to raise the spirits of a disillusioned nation!"

It was then revealed how BIMMO 10314 was a media project aimed to produce a graphic novel targeted for all ages, but particularly the younger audiences. This graphic novel would first be premiered as an online series with a regular weekly release. After its completion, the novel would be marketed as a printed publication for a relatively cheap price. As a government production, it was supposed to be free. However, since their counterpart in the printing business, the Bureau of Print Industry (or BPI), had issues to contend with, BIMMO resorted to contracting a private printing firm to expedite the process. In exchange, the firm asked for mere "recoup" of their marketing expenses, supposedly to ensure that the book will reach the right shelves. BIMMO shoulders the cost of printing itself.

"We've got six months to do this," Seo ended with the same enthusiasm she has been holding up throughout the video, "From there, we can expect to produce a future nation full of hope and pride! This is the Bureau of Information Management and Media Operations. Where there is knowledge, there is power."

As the screen retreated, Dakila opened the floor for any comments or questions. Noticing that none wanted to take his offer, he called out to the administrative staff to distribute the employees' respective contracts. During the distribution, the supervisor continued to explain that the project was supposed to be finished already. Then again, six months in, they have not gone beyond the drawing board. Since the budget cycle went for an annual basis, BIMMO had to show at least a semblance of the results before the year ends. Else, not only would the project be scrapped, BIMMO would be candidate for significant budget reductions the following year for being unable to meet some, if not all, of the objectives the bureau itself has set. As much as the government wanted to fund everything, there were limited resources to reckon with, especially as financing was diverted to priority sectors such as health and the economy.

Most of the employees did not even listen to what Dakila had to say. They immediately signed their contracts and walked back to their posts. All but Aurelio stayed behind.

"What is it, Geine?" Dakila asked, "Anything you've got in mind?"

"Sir," Aurelio kept his eyes on the contract, "This doesn't look like the terms we've agreed on in the interview."

Dakila walks toward Aurelio's seat, "What do you mean?"

"Like here," Aurelio points to one of the contract clauses, "I'm supposed to receive an equivalent of Salary Grade 14, but the contract states that it's Salary Grade 12."

The salary grade scale in the civil service provided a simplified standard to determine the basic pay a government employee would receive. Salary Grade 1 was the lowest, which was essentially the same amount as minimum wage. The government increased these wages by law.

"Uh, yeah, but since you're hired on a contractual basis, you're having a 20% additional to your basic salary. So, it's still equivalent to Salary Grade 14, if you think about it. Maybe even more."

"I don't know… This sounds like a demotion. I received Salary Grade 16 in my last job."

"Hmm… You know what? What if we discuss this with the admin staff?"

Aurelio flipped the pages of the contract, "I don't think they'd like to see me demanding about something that involves what they do, sir. It's just that, well, I noticed how I'm turning out to be the lowest paid among the *senior writers* here."

Santoria had a wage equivalent to Salary Grade 15, while the other two writers had Salary Grade 16. Since all of them were contracted, they also receive the premium Aurelio would be having.

While Dakila could only give a thin smile, Aurelio continued, "Anyway, how about this job description? Forgive me for bringing this up, but almost none of these had anything to do with the secret project you've introduced a while ago."

"Nah," Dakila replied with a pat on Aurelio's back, "Basically, it's me and CAS giving the orders around here. Didn't you see the last entry? Don't worry about it. Are you thinking we're going to airdrop you to Waziristan just to gather material?"

"M-maybe?"

"Ridiculous! In fact, I'm having you take a week working from home. Starting tomorrow."

Aurelio removed his attention from the contract for a while, "Wait, why?! What have I done, sir?"

"Nothing. Nothing, really. It's just that, since you're new here, we still haven't got you some equipment to use. You know, for writing and stuff. You did tell us you don't have your own? Besides, we couldn't always assemble in the office with all these mass gathering restrictions."

"T-that's correct, sir…"

Dakila then whispered, "If you're worried about Ma'am Seo's timeline, don't think of it. With the staff we have, we simply can't release weekly. I'll fill you in later how we'll do it."

Even when Aurelio had not yet signed his contract, Dakila seemed positive that they would be working together. Thus, despite the hazy details, Aurelio decided to sign anyway. After all, he needed the job. Meanwhile, the rest of the day was quite uneventful. It proved to be routine activity, none of which appeared to be driving the top secret mission they were supposed to be working on for half a year already.

An unbeliever of the correlation between overtime and productivity, Aurelio took his sling bag and quietly left the office. Not far behind him jogged Santoria, who carried a small backpack with her. She tapped him, but he did not respond.

"Geine," she smiled, "Why don't we go home together, just like we used to do?"

"I don't know you," Aurelio grinds his teeth, "Have you heard of social distancing?"

"But… But we're going to work from home for a while. I'd miss you."

"I couldn't care less about that. Now, if you'll excuse me."

"There's more of those incriminating evidence from where they came from," Santoria muttered, "If you don't agree with me now…"

He shot a fiery look at her, "This society may favor women like you, but I'm ready."

Sensing his aggression, she eventually allowed Aurelio to go ahead without her.

With a wide smile she hid beneath her mask, Santoria thought with utmost thrill, "It's the first time we talked in a long time. I can't believe it's really working. Too bad, he didn't agree. Time for Phase 2, then."

Work from home. Telecommuting. Long distance work. There were many names for a similar concept. In order to alleviate the significant increase of daytime populations in the city, the government has decided to officially adopt work from home measures, albeit the information and communication technology (ICT) infrastructure appeared quite unprepared to handle it. In some areas where work from home was adopted in a wider scale, workers had to contend with slower internet connections, frequent telecom system fixes, energy failures, and the necessity to always find charging spots. Traffic, among other things, was still not alleviated. It had only transferred from analog to digital. Besides, there were professions wherein work from home might not exactly be applicable in the first place, and for those who still take the high road, traffic congestion remained.

This was the first time in his government experience where Aurelio worked from home. Surely, it allowed flexibility to manage your own time. Plus, you acquired the perquisites of living it in your own home. What he realized soon enough was the invasive nature of any job. It was called *occupation*, after all. From the standard nine-to-five, Aurelio found himself working 24/7. The messages just kept on pouring in every e-mail and social media account he operated. Some preferred to contact at 3 PM, while others chose 3 AM. Every hour must be checked, even in your sleep. At times, he could not even determine the distinction between a task, a favor, and a parody. Personal communications mixed with professional communications so well, nothing seemed to be quite personal anymore. If one took it personally though, checkmate.

There was even a debate sparked by one of his coworkers on the difference of graphic novels and manga. Both were serialized, and both seemed to utilize similar art forms. Dakila had no say. Apparently, he was busy with other matters. Only when the debate dragged on did Chief Seo enter the conversation. In the end, most of them agreed that calling it a manga may run counter against the nationalistic aims of their project because it specifically applied to the Japanese style of telling stories. Besides, the government might have not approved it at all if they billed the production as such. While there were many artists out there who agreed accepting contracts and commissions for the right price, the right price was usually on the high end of the spectrum. The creative industry was taking the world by storm, yet the government was not too keen on throwing its hat in the ring through partnerships with these relatively competitive private firms. More than efficiency and effectiveness, a financially-struggling institution aimed for economy regardless of importance.

"Oh, Geine? You're here? You can still take the rest of the week off, right?"

A surprised Dakila, who somehow neglected to wear his mask in their mildly spacious office, welcomed the early Aurelio on a Monday morning.

"Let's just say, er, I wanted to get into the zone."

In reality, Aurelio had not found the work from home scheme too appealing. The implementation may have been a factor, but somehow, he only thought that it was people who still control the technology. No matter how high technology went, if humanity could not hope to keep up the pace, it would still tend to create more problems than solutions. Besides, since Santoria began to know his contact details through the group chat, he had been relentlessly been receiving messages from her. He figured he needed a break from the obsessed debacle.

"Miss Santoria's not here?" Aurelio pointed to her cubicle.

Dakila's eyes narrowed, "You're not telling me you miss her now, are you?"

"Sir Red, I already cleared this up for you!"

"I kid, of course. She's with one of our illustrators to gather material. You know, the project."

"Is that so? I might have missed that."

Dakila laughed heartily, "See? You really do miss her!"

As Aurelio got his head caught by his supervisor's arm, he could only sigh, "If she loves me, how would she unlove me?"

Am I Appealing To You?

"Do you think this would be appealing?"

Arya Bernice Santoria, 26 years of age, gazed at the façade of an old settlement built by colonizers centuries ago. It was, of course, a shadow of its former self. Only the imposing gate and the disconnected parts of the stone walls remained intact, all of which were invaded slowly by crawling flora.

"What are you referring to? The place where we stand or the place in his heart?"

Pulling that quip was her companion, the male illustrator Rene Goncalves. With a phone in hand to take pictures and notes, 40-year-old Goncalves put up a mischievous smile which appeared out of line with his plain and inconspicuous clothing.

"Where'd that come from? I'm serious here, Rene," Santoria fired back as she typed on her phone.

"Nothing much," Goncalves shrugged, "I just want to go home."

"Aren't you worried if we really don't finish this on time?"

"Of course. But I've been working in the government for ten years now. Even without BIMMO, someone somewhere will offer me something. Even during this crisis."

"Come on, cooperate for once. I'm thinking if this kind of setting will suit our story?"

"You want to know what I think?"

Santoria did not respond, but the illustrator continued anyway, "It's full of trash. Why does it have to be original anyway? The chief knows better. It'd be easier if we copy some successful story out there, put in our own touch, and release. They won't know the difference! Besides, have you seen anyone read a manga because of the plot?"

"We've already agreed that this isn't a manga," Santoria said with some irritation, "And no. I've written stories before, but what I realized is how liberal we've been with settings. We can spend five or ten pages describing something, and still fall short with the actual thing."

"Wow," disbelief being apparent all over Goncalves's face, "You're quite inspired just now. What's happening?"

She sighed before walking ahead of him, "Never mind that. Let's go."

He bended over to look up, "Finally!"

Then again, another train of thought occupied Santoria's mind. Provided this project would be unsuccessful, it was likely that their contracts would be terminated and they would part ways. When that happens, she might not have another good opportunity to become closer to Aurelio. God knew what would come next. She should carefully lay the groundwork for her personal top secret mission. Back in the office, Aurelio had been gladly showing off his ideas to their supervisor while the rest of the team were gone.

"An interesting plot," Dakila commented, "but our demographic is for all ages. You can't just be an educational medium. You have to be entertaining, too."

"But sir," Aurelio countered, "isn't the joy of learning the greatest joy of them all? Happiness comes from knowing, and sadness from not knowing. It's the government's job to educate…"

The supervisor waves his hands up and down, "No offense, but that won't do. We're already halfway the project. We can't make any radical changes."

Of course, Dakila did not mean that statement. They have not even released anything yet.

With gleaming eyes, Aurelio looked at his supervisor, "Sir Red, I know this is feasible. Our generation isn't about the aesthetics only. We're into form and substance."

Dakila pulled out his laptop and browsed some statistics, "Well, that's not what our beta readers say. Apparently, it depends more on the genre than the plot itself. It's like…"

"What? You've got beta readers?"

"Sure. Alpha, beta, gamma, delta. We've got them. But basically, it's my child's class in high school. There are about 40 of them."

"Wait, you mean to tell me, you're having these kids involved in a *top secret project*?!"

"Geine, don't act so surprised," the supervisor laughed, "We're in the media! Nothing is truly top secret in our league. Not even those shady keyboard warriors some have been allegedly using."

With Aurelio dumbfounded, Dakila patted his back, "Listen, it's just Ma'am Seo's way to pull some legs in the government. You can't convince them by saying, 'Hey, we've got some cool idea.' Heck, many of us have *cool* ideas. Why don't you ask them?"

"Who…?"

All three writers and two illustrators have returned from their respective field work. Other than Santoria and Goncalves, there was another illustrator, and two more writers. The latter Aurelio did not seem to remember from his first week. Dakila would only explain that since they were *borrowed* to work on a part-time basis with BIMMO, they were not expected to physically report every day. It turned out they work directly under the nation's president.

Dakila leaned back, "So, how goes Monaco?"

"Sir Red," Goncalves rolled a dice to the supervisor's direction, "Is that the only place worth going for you?"

They did not really go to Monaco, but apparently, it had become Dakila's pet phrase.

"Of course! But enough about me. It's almost two weeks and we still haven't released anything. CAS will be furious."

Everyone looked at each other as they consciously removed their masks, waiting on who will speak first. Then, smiles began to shine one by one. Before long, all of them were sending signals for Aurelio to facilitate.

"I'm sorry, Geine," Dakila sympathized, "It seems the democratic process has decided."

Aurelio frowned, "Sir? Seriously, I know next to nothing! How can I...?"

One of the writers remarked, "As Buddha once said, when you know nothing, you know everything. You can do it, boy."

The other writer beside him nudged, "You idiot! It was Confucius who said that."

The one nudged pulled out his phone and swiped to search for the quote to prove the point, "I've got a ton of memes here. I'm pretty sure it's Gautama Buddha."

"Please," Aurelio pleaded, "let's get back to the topic..."

"Geine's right," Santoria interjected as she forwarded a file in their chat group, "Here are the revised proposals I've made since the last beta reviews came in."

The list boiled down to three major narrative proposals. The first story would revolve around a slice of life romance which used daily experiences as links to nationalistic tendencies. The second story involves a super spy romance that almost bordered the science fiction and fantasy classification. The third story was a historical romance which may not be historically accurate, but would be set in the colonial period, shortly before the revolution overthrowing the colonizers.

"Okay...," Dakila raised his hand, "Let's have a vote."

The vote led to a deadlock, however. The proposals had two votes each. Only Aurelio had not yet voted, and thus, their attention shifted back to him once more.

"Well," Santoria looked intently at Aurelio's eyes, as if in search for something within them, "am I appealing to you?"

Dakila wore his mask to hide his chuckle as Santoria corrected herself, "I mean, is anything appealing to you?"

Aurelio's face contorted a little for a while before answering, "Uh, I guess... D-does it all have to be romance? Where's the grand narrative? The love for the nation?"

"I tried, okay? But when will you appreciate my love…?"

"Come again?"

"Love for the nation! It's not something that can be grasped too easily. Chief said it herself, it's an imagined community. If we are to love the nation together, we have to love each other first."

Just then, Goncalves gave Santoria a light push towards Aurelio's spot, "Come on, you lot! Kiss and make up already!"

"Oh, I see where this is going," Aurelio rubbed his chin, "Stop it already, Miss Santoria. I'm fed up by your crazy antics."

"Ooh, tough luck, Arya," Goncalves whispered to Santoria, who ignored him.

"As I was saying," Aurelio perused the proposals again, "Okay, I'm good with romance if that's what the beta audience has been recommending. Personally though, I'd like it to be set in a historical period where we have more liberty. The colonial period is pretty much recorded, and their structures remain today. It'd be difficult for us to balance accuracy and creativity."

Dakila asked with some interest, "What do you have in mind then?"

Aurelio then described a story set in the precolonial period, where there was a budding romance between two lovers who were far apart in the societal ladder. However, it would not be the traditional Romeo and

Juliet approach. It would be presented that they were actually adept in their respective fields, contributing service to the community may it be small or great. Since there would be little to add to the records currently available of the precolonial period, greater liberties could be utilized, such as placing anachronistic elements to make the story more relatable to many, without much ado to the accuracy of details.

"What's more," Aurelio added, "we can use an approach rarely used here, but has been quite successful elsewhere in Asia and Europe. It'd be both educational and fun, right?"

"Geine," Goncalves folded his arms, "I'm pretty sure it's a good idea for you. But how about us? What model can we copy from to work on the character designs, the backgrounds?"

"Oh, don't worry about that," Aurelio sent a bunch of files as he responded, "Look at this codex. You can use this for the character designs. I also summarized accounts describing places in great detail for you to have something to work on with the setting. For reference, here are some places outside the country which have similar architecture. But feel free to do your own style, in my opinion."

"Hey, these aren't half-bad," Goncalves showed some of the opened files to his fellow illustrator, "I can't imagine those ancient people were actually working with such a rich color palette."

Dakila turned to the rest of the team, "If everyone's okay with this, then let's get to work."

At first, there was murmuring. Then, there was nodding. It seemed Aurelio's proposal got the go signal. Starting from almost zero, they worked in overdrive to have some output for Seo's approval. Since they did not have much time to spare, overtime was needed for the next few days, and eyebags formed layers upon layers. However, Aurelio was not having any of it. He left before everyone else, not entirely by choice, but primarily because he had the farthest residence from the BIMMO office. While Dakila understood this situation, the rest of the team did not appreciate the seemingly preferential treatment from their supervisor as much.

"Geine, a minute please," Santoria visited Aurelio in his cubicle.

"No, I'm busy," he replied without even looking at her, "Won't spare you even a second."

"I want to know where you based these characters from. You know, a writer to writer exchange."

"Are you mocking me? Don't you think I know you? You're the famous online author Aris in Wunderland. Your romance stories have gained millions of reads worldwide. Surely, you've got more experience than I on this matter."

Santoria's pen name, Aris in Wunderland (pronounced as *ah reese*, not *ah rise*), has earned some notoriety in the webnovel world. Her works such as the *Repentance of Healer*, *The World the Two of Us Only Knows*, *Operation Seeing You Again*, *The Princess Rejects All the Charming Ones*, and *A Lovely Spy Follows You in Another World* have been published online and in print. Nearing a billion reads in the web and with millions of copies sold throughout the years, Aris in Wunderland was a local sensation, and yet, not many people knew it was actually Santoria who crafted them behind the scenes.

"You researched me, eh? I'm flattered."

"Don't be. It just helped me to dislike you more."

Sadness filled Santoria, "Come on, don't tease me like that. I mean, sure, it's earned me some fans, and maybe some money from royalties, but when I saw your plot… Look, here's something interesting. Research-based, and yet, I can already feel the story flowing within me."

"See, you know it already? Now, get lost. I don't want you ruining my life again. Ever."

She retreated to her cubicle still downcast. None of her tactics appear to be affecting him one bit. Soon enough, it was review day with Seo herself in the conference room. The two part-time writers were working on urgent presidential communications, leaving Dakila, Aurelio, and Santoria to face their chief.

Without much of a reaction on her face, Seo quickly read their initial output, "Hmm. Not bad. The story actually seems to be just the subtle nationalistic type we've been looking for. Not too pushy, but it lingers. Don't you think so, too, Red?"

"Y-yes, ma'am," Dakila straightened up due to tension, "The beta readers seem to like it more than the past ones we've worked on. They say it can actually help in their studies."

"Wait, they really mind that aspect?"

"Maybe because Social Studies is among the most difficult to master for them?"

"Actually, I'm talking about the chemistry here. It's like right from the get-go, you'll already root for the would-be couple. Even if you don't, at least you're fine about them being together anyway. But…"

Dakila gulped, while the two writers begun to be nervous as well.

"Arya," Seo continued, "I don't see much of your style here. I somehow feel this is more of Geine's work. You've convinced me with this storyline, but it has to be coherent all the way."

"Yes, Chief," Santoria nodded.

"Hmm. No offense, Geine. You've got good premise on this one, but here's the deal. I'm realigning your assignments, okay? Geine, I'll pair you with Arya."

Aurelio opened his mouth and raised his index finger as an attempt to dissuade Seo, but the BIMMO Chief has already made up her mind.

"Look, I can't have two pairs working on different projects. We tried that before, and it doesn't work. Besides, Arya's the bestselling author here. Learn from her techniques. You can still gather material with the illustrators, but in the main, you have to work closer together considering our tight schedule. Got it?"

"Yes, ma'am," all of them responded.

Seo nodded, "Alright, good job. Get back to work."

As they departed the room, Santoria made a quick glance at Seo, who in turn gave her a wink.

With Seo out of sight, Dakila sighed and pumped his fist, "You nailed it, Geine. Oh my, I can't believe we're running our first issue this early. Really!"

Aurelio bowed, "I'm glad it worked for us, sir. But, I'm still bothered."

"By what?"

"Her," Aurelio pointed at the smiling Santoria.

She inched closer to Aurelio and softly said, "Aww, I still love you, okay?"

Avoiding her gaze, Aurelio scratched his head, "That's not what I have in mind. And please wear your mask."

"Maybe so," Santoria thought to herself as she followed his request, "How would you love me, then?"

Draw Me Closer, Never Let Me Go

"Looks like most of the comments go down more on the art style than the story itself."

Goncalves scrolled the feed of the first chapters they released online. The graphic novel, entitled *Kris at Kampilan*, followed the budding love story of Kris, a sophisticated girl of high societal status named after the asymmetrical blade, and Kampilan, a simple slave boy named after the single-edged, double-pointed sword, during the precolonial period. In particular, a time when foreigners have been pouring in their area, and the local powers expanding their spheres of influence. Their personalities supposedly reflect the nature of the weapons they were named after, but somehow, the audiences were buying the seemingly generic plot.

"No kidding. They're even saying the characters are too well-covered considering the time frame," the other illustrator read the comments on her tablet, "I bet if they knew this was a work of Aris in Wunderland, everyone would go crazy about it."

This female illustrator wearing a blouse top and pants was Listy Charm Montemayor, aged 28. She is more adept than Goncalves in terms of digital technology, and her main task was to convert Goncalves's raw black and white sketches into the final form in color. Since BIMMO did not have much equipment to work with, Montemayor had to bring some of her own for convenience, including the tablet she was holding. It functioned both as a drawing tablet and, when docked with a keyboard, as a laptop.

"No," Goncalves said, "It's Geine. If only you saw how inspired Arya is now because of him…"

"I thought they broke up already? I was there."

"I won't be so sure about that. It looks like a high school romance to me."

"What do you mean?"

Goncalves rolled his eyes, "You know, LQ now, then they go back together later. Age doesn't really matter for things like that."

For starters, LQ meant love quarrel.

"I don't know how you see it that way," Montemayor pointed a pen at him before drawing a chart, "If you analyze what relationships Geine have been developing in our team so far, you can easily see that the one he's most interested in now is… is…"

Upon finishing the quick sketch, she was flustered.

"The result…?" Goncalves tried to peer on her work.

"Don't mind that, Rene," Montemayor pulled the chart away, "I… I'll have to review for our next chapter, okay?"

The following week, Aurelio could still be seen busy typing the storyboard on the secondhand laptop provided for by BIMMO. The ideas were really flowing for him. He simply did not have time to stop, else there might be no other good chance. Besides, he did not want to take the overtime, not when his fixed salary job provided no overtime pay. Suddenly, a cold breeze sent chills to his one arm.

"Here you go," someone handed him a drink.

"Did you disinfect this?" Aurelio frowned, "I didn't order anything."

"I know. You don't order anything," the person smiled, "Don't worry. It's on me."

Only when he turned to see who it was did his complexion become pale. It was Montemayor.

With hands clasped, Aurelio knelt, "I'm sorry about that first day, okay?! Please, spare me!"

"What are you saying? I'm here for the next chapter."

"What next chapter?"

"Of our lives."

"Who?"

She spread her arms, "*Kris at Kampilan.*"

"Oh, yes, right," Aurelio returned to his seat and shifted his laptop for Montemayor to see the screen, "Here, Listy. I was thinking if I can already execute the plot device Miss Santoria rejected for the first chapter. It's nice to introduce the hurdles Kris and Kampilan have to face for their love of each other, but there has to be an explosive incident early on."

Montemayor squinted, "Is that Zheng He?"

"Hey, good eye," he laughs a bit, "but not really him. I just want you to use him as a model for the foreign commissioner I'm planning to meddle with Kris and Kampilan's kingdom affairs."

"Wouldn't that make the story look like a Wuxia series?"

"Nonsense! This novel is still about nationalism. If there's no common enemy they can unite against, their kingdom will just squabble and divide among themselves."

"Your thinking is too advanced, Geine. We won't want to place a foreign country in bad light, especially a present ally nation. Can't it be just a neighboring kingdom or something?"

"Listy, this is a government production. We can't portray something that suggests discord from within. On the personal level, maybe, but not on the national level."

"Seeing the comments though," Montemayor pulled out her phone, "some are debating whether it really had something to do with the concept of nation."

"It doesn't, but at least it got them talking about it, right?"

"Um, yeah, sure... Speaking of talk, maybe you could, you know. It's the weekend and..."

Aurelio tilted his head, "You want to work on it tomorrow?"

"Yes, with you, if possible."

He checked his phone, "Sure, it's you and Rene, right?"

She looked away, "Y-yeah... Let's meet at this place, alright?"

The work week seemed to fly and it was already the weekend. Aurelio was early in the place Montemayor indicated, a restaurant café with free and reliable Wi-Fi, as well as open air dining. While it was quite far from their office, it proved to be a nearer destination for them. Looking out the window, he saw Montemayor alight a Transportation Network Vehicle Service (TNVS) car, but it was only her. She wore a blouse that flowed down to her knees, wrapped by a large belt around her waist. Her purse she carried on her hand while its slim handle was only placed loosely on her shoulder. A small headband with a flower attached to it had been neatly resting on her head. It was not that she had long hair, which only went down a little past her shoulders, but she did not seem to have used it when she was at the office.

"Where's Rene?" the masked Aurelio asked, expecting an obvious answer.

"He's got some errands," Montemayor reasoned, "I think it's got something to do with his aerobics classes."

Goncalves also worked as a part-time aerobics instructor, which kept him relatively fit for someone his age. The government usually disallowed income from other sources, but somehow, contractual employees such as they were given some sort of privilege to juggle outside jobs.

"I see," Aurelio brought out the handwritten notes from his bag, "Let's get to it then."

"Please, let me say this first."

"What?"

"Do you really have to wear the same kind of outfit? We're not in the office, you know?"

He rubbed his chin, "Hmm. It's more for the production team. If they'd relive my simple life in film or in TV, at least they won't have to modify their wardrobe too much. An affordable character, yes?"

She gave a forced laugh while looking at her own clothing, "Ah, is that so? Well, it's just that, maybe, you know…"

"But between you and me," he said softly, "These are the best ones I've got. I come from a background of poverty, see, and…"

A blushing Montemayor hushed him, "It's alright. Your best is good enough. So, have you ordered anything?"

"Uh…," Aurelio slowly retrieved the menu by his side, "How do I put this…?"

She reached out for his hand holding the menu, "You really don't order anything, do you? I don't mind. It's on me today, okay?"

"But…"

"No, I'm the one who requested this anyway."

He pulled his hand away, giving Montemayor a slight surprise.

"A-alright, your call, then."

She hailed a waiter, who wore adequate personal protective equipment, and witnessing how Montemayor easily places the orders, Aurelio thought she must have been a regular customer in that joint. It did not take long before the orders arrived, which did not interrupt Aurelio one bit when he discussed his plans for the novel. Montemayor listened intently, her hand supporting her slightly tilting head.

"Tell me," she remarked, "is it really your first time working on a fictional work like this? You seem very skilled at this."

"Thanks," he replied without looking at her, "To be honest, it is. At least, after my long hiatus."

The last statement piqued her interest, "What do you mean?"

Aurelio smirked, "You'd really not want to hear it. So, about this scene…"

"I'm interested," she lightly slammed the papers in front of him, "Please?"

He looked at her, revealing a frowning face, "You won't tell the others at BIMMO?"

She shook her head.

"Fine," Aurelio sighed, "simply put, I have works in almost every medium that involves writing."

"Novels? Novellas? Stories?"

"Yup."

"Poems? Haiku?"

"Sure."

"Plays? Songs?"

"I still carry one of them with me."

Her eyes twinkled for a moment, "Really? Can I see?"

Hesitantly, he pulled out a small piece of paper from his wallet. The edges were quite chipped, but the paper itself was still intact. Nonetheless, the years have taken its toll on the material.

"It's just the lyrics, though."

However, she has been engrossed enough on the lyrics to ignore Aurelio's explanation.

Montemayor asked, "So, how do you exactly sing this piece?"

He tried a few lines, and then his voice cracked, causing him to have a few coughs, which caused some of the people around them to look. She gave him a drink to relieve his throat. Aurelio had not given the song justice, as far as Montemayor saw it. Thus, upon absorbing the tune with which he sang it, she went with her own attempt.

"W-wow…," Aurelio gaped at the sight of Montemayor's performance, "I know the song's bad, but your voice, it's just… You're a really great singer, Listy!"

Soon enough, they realized how a few of the customers in the café were actually watching her sing. It was an original piece, so they were somehow curious of what she just sang. Her masked face only added to the mystery.

"I-it's nothing, really… I just took voice lessons."

"No way."

"But Geine, I couldn't have sung this nicely if the song itself is no good," she raised the paper in her hand, "You should know better. It's like me drawing the novel without your input."

He quickly takes the paper away from her, and hides it back in his wallet.

"Anyway… I'm still just two releases ahead in this storyline. And because of Ma'am Seo, I still have to get Miss Santoria's approval of them instead of just Sir Red's. So yeah, whatever we've discussed here is still subject to change."

Pointing at his notes, Aurelio continued, "I suggest you can do these scenes in advance. That's what I think both of them will like, but don't take my word for it. Just do it at your own pace."

"Alright," she answers with a disinterested look, "but is that the only thing Arya's approving in your life?"

"Come again?"

Montemayor leaned closer, "At this very moment, Arya's eyes are on us. Be careful."

An alerted Aurelio looked around, but she grabbed his arm to stop him from acting up.

"That wretched Santoria! We're never really a couple, but why is she acting like we are?!"

"A-about that... Geine..."

Noticing her change in tone, Aurelio's attention went back to Montemayor, who released her hold of his arm at about the same moment.

"Weeks since that breakup," she sadly recounted, "I got to know you better. And, it's been fun, really. How else could I put this...? I'm sorry."

"Wait, why?"

"Even if we're interacting well in the office, I know you still harbor that bad first day experience. This may not be on behalf of the rest of the girls, but as for me, I apologize for judging too quickly and all. Do you forgive me?"

Wide-eyed, Aurelio could only say, "That escalated quickly."

Meeting his eyes were Montemayor's gleaming ones, "Geine?"

"Alright, alright. It's not like it's worth much...," he assured her as he prepared to keep his notes, "I forgive you, but why tell me here? Now?"

"If I do this in the office, do you think they'd let me off the hook? Rumors will spread that you're hitting me shortly after breaking Arya's heart. That's why I use the consultation sessions we casually do to draw you closer, to not let you go, and yes, to know the truth."

"But if Arya's watching now, wouldn't she...?"

"She won't. Right now, I'm her important ally and friend. Would you believe it? From her perspective, I'm just grinding information out of you. Nothing more."

"What information?"

"She knows you don't like to talk to her. So, she turned to me for help, because it looks like I'm the one you're being quite keen to talk with."

"Oh, that," Aurelio gave a nervous laugh, "I just noticed how Rene's close with Miss Santoria, so I figured if I'm to do this job well, I should at least have working relations with you."

Montemayor folded her legs, "You're brutally honest. Okay, I'll drop this one time."

"Y-yes?"

"Do you love Arya?"

He showed his empty palms, "Never did, never will."

She looked at his hands, and then at his eyes, "Well then. What would it take for you to be in love?"

We Never Learn

"He didn't really answer anything that might help."

This was what Montemayor related to Santoria later on, emphasizing how Aurelio was more interested in his career than anything else. After all, what excitement he displayed explaining the details of the graphic novel, it did not reflect as much when it came to talking about his personal life.

"So," Santoria pondered, "a woman who shares his core beliefs, is that it?"

"Basically, that's just it," Montemayor replied, "Come on, Arya. That's just a flimsy excuse."

"No. I think that's just typical of him. You might not have realized it yet, but Geine's one of the more faithful people you'll meet."

"If that's the case, he doesn't look like the religious type. I really don't know what you liked about him, but I have work to do, alright?"

Santoria let her be. In her mind, however, there was one upcoming event that may well be useful in her overall campaign. It did not take long before their supervisor announces it to them.

Dakila told the team, "We've got a three-day seminar at Hotel del Luna."

"Sir," one of the part-time writers commented, "We're not departed spirits! We're not returning from the dead, are we?!"

Dakila laughed, "Of course, I'm kidding. But the three-day seminar is real. It's at Hotel Pastoria, and whether you like it or you like it, we're all coming. It'd have been nice if it's Hotel de Paris Monte-Carlo, but…"

Aurelio raised his hand, which Dakila acknowledged.

"Sir Red," Aurelio said, "May I be excused?"

"Why?"

"I still have a backlog in my story. I'd prefer focusing on it as a skeletal force in the office. Besides, mass gatherings should be prohibited unless the participants are immunized."

Montemayor patted Aurelio at the back, "All participants should be vaccinated though. They have safety protocols. Knowing you, Geine, you're just thinking of the expenses, aren't you? Considering Pastoria is as far as the Land of Oz…"

"Don't worry about that," the supervisor assured, "This time, BIMMO will fund us. Well, partly. Pastoria is a 5-star hotel. We'd still have to share rooms."

"You can have the rooms, sir," Aurelio entered, "I could at least help reduce public spending…"

"We're already reserved," Dakila showed a crudely prepared sheet with the room assignments.

The seminar was for communication teams from various agencies all over the country, each having representatives, but most sending less than what BIMMO intended to sponsor. Then again, simply put, BIMMO being the national-level agency for communications should at least have a sizeable contingent. Seo and Dakila would have single, exclusive rooms. Those who would share rooms are as follows: the two part-time writers, Montemayor and Santoria, Aurelio and Goncalves. All of them did not have issues with the seminar. They were even eyeing more on the hotel's amenities than what the seminar had to offer. All of them except Aurelio.

"Let me get this straight, sir," Aurelio queried, "This seminar can be credited as training and development, right?"

Aside from experience, relevant training was also considered as criteria of qualification for higher government positions.

Dakila nodded while typing on his phone, "Sure. It's equivalent to 30 hours."

It struck Aurelio. For the first time, he would be able to gain one more key to his career in the civil service. Who knew then? With that training in his resume, he could probably overcome contractualization and become a suitable candidate for regularization.

"Alright, sir. What do I need to prepare?"

"Nothing much. Just learn and enjoy."

Apparently, he did not take heed of his supervisor's words. As the team assembled at the airport, they found Aurelio carrying one of the larger bags among them. Only Seo's was bigger, but it did not have much content. The chief was allotting space for what she would shop at Pastoria. Unlike Seo's, Aurelio's bag proved to be quite heavy when one of them tried carrying it. While it iwas nowhere near heavy enough to exceed the limit, they only wondered what was inside the bag.

"I... I'm weight training," was what he said to justify the heavy luggage.

In reality, he did not want to come unready. It should be making sense. To the rest of the team, however, he just appeared to be preparing too much. All of these thoughts vanished with the relatively short flight. Despite experiencing turbulence along the way, and the somewhat cramped space for passengers who were supposed to be distanced safely from each other, the plane landed safely at the airport. From there, a Hotel Pastoria mini-bus was waiting to fetch them. It did not look spacious enough when filled with passengers, but as for Aurelio, he did what he can to avoid sitting anywhere near Santoria.

Montemayor whispered to Santoria during their trip, "Just give it up, will you? You're not getting back together at this rate."

"How can you tell?", Santoria softly shot back, "God Himself made us meet again even when I thought it's impossible."

"Don't appropriate something to a higher being just because you think it's for you. It'd be better for you to focus on the project, just like Geine. You know what's at stake here."

"You're charming when you don't mean what you say, Charm."

"When will you ever learn?"

"Indeed, we never learn," Santoria smiled.

As soon as they arrived at the venue, the BIMMO personnel went straight to the event. Despite being a national event, it did not seem to hold to its promise. For the most part, it was an uneventful affair. Participants could be seen openly yawning, heavily using their phones, and taking their good time in the comfort rooms. That is, until BIMMO itself presented its case. Knowing how sedated the rest of the participants were due to the earlier presentations, Chief Seo decided to ditch the original one she prepared and use 10314 instead to spice things up.

"Damn!" Dakila typed frantically on his phone, "Get ready for trouble! And make it double!"

At first, the rest of the team did not exactly understand what their supervisor was getting at. However, with Seo just a few minutes into her presentation, a question from one of the senior officials in the audience was raised. She ignored the official because it was not yet time for interpellation, but the old man was adamant. He stood up, took a microphone for himself, and confronted Seo in the midst of an awakened crowd.

Clad in a jacket indicating his workplace, the senior official jeers, "Is this the best we can do for a national agency like BIMMO?! Heck, my grandchild can draft a better project than 10314!"

This little display triggered the BIMMO Chief, "Oh, yeah?! Tell me, what have you done to raise nationalism through the media?!"

"Simple," he laughed rather mischievously, "Playing the national anthem, putting up flags everywhere, fervent marching and military training, inculcating love of country from a young age through intense combos of theory and practice, distributing symbolic materials that will remind of one's home country, and many more. We have to invest in our people, and to invest heavily is the only way to go!"

"If your intention is to create *blind following*, then I won't stop you."

Most of the people present did not understand Seo's counterpoint, but the senior official knew, and it sent him fuming mad.

"You ungrateful sod! I tell you, that's nothing more than a novelty project! It won't take off!"

"Wouldn't it? As we speak, the graphic novel is earning thousands of reads online! When we finish the series and publish it, we will not only recoup initial expenses, we would potentially double the reach of our medium. The objectives are on their track of being achieved. Now then, which is more nationalistic?"

The senior official dropped the mike, and walked out with a few others who are apparently his companions. Meanwhile, Seo's eyes wandered, and then she spoke.

"Creativity and innovation isn't something you can force on anybody. If you think our children are stuck in the Stone Age, then so be it! But as far as data shows, the Stone Age did not end with the shortage of stones. We clearly present a good solution. Let the evidence speak for themselves. I won't even ask if you agree with me. Thank you, this ends my presentation."

Thereafter, the angered chief departed in haste. Her mind was filled with rage, and it was just on the first day of the seminar, so much so that she forgot to bring any of her things. Dakila rushed to fix everything for her, but nothing seemed to be able to keep her in Pastoria. As soon as the seminar ended for the day, the BIMMO team learned of the inevitable outcome: Seo took the return flight earlier than scheduled. This presented a dilemma for their logistical setup, which the supervisor explained over dinner at the hotel.

"You see," Dakila opened, "The situation goes like this. Without CAS, I can't keep the other single bedroom. So, I'll have to move in with one of the twin bedrooms."

"Well, sir," Aurelio responded, "That doesn't sound so bad…"

"Err, yes… Except the fact that we got the extra room because of the two exclusive ones. So, basically, three of us have to move out."

"Wait," Goncalves asked with a grin on his face, "you mean seven people would have to be stuck in two rooms? What of safety protocols?"

"As you say," Dakila surrendered.

The illustrator enthusiastically raised his hand, "I first dibs the boys' room!"

Aurelio stood up, "Hey, that's not fair, Rene! You mean I get to go to the girls' room?!"

"Keep your voice down, will you? Don't tell me you're scared of two mean girls?"

Montemayor and Santoria let it slide.

"It's not a matter of personality than of morality. If there's no other way, then I propose that I take my leave, Sir Red!"

Dakila could only shake his head as he witnessed Aurelio walk out of their dinner, "Oh, no. Here we go again…"

It took only a few minutes before Aurelio was ready to leave the hotel, until he was hindered once more as he approached the exit. It was not the supervisor, nor any person in particular. A heavy downpour has hampered all transport options for him at that moment. With thunder and lightning storming the background, all he could logically do would be to sit it out in the hotel lobby. As he was nodding off while seated due to boredom from hours of waiting for the weather to improve, he was approached by a familiar figure.

"M-Miss Santoria?" he weakly asked while half-awake.

She smiled and handed him a keycard, "Wondering if this is a dream or something?"

Incomprehensible words came out of his mouth as soon as he dropped the keycard. At least for Aurelio, it made some sense, but Santoria did not catch a thing from what he was saying. Despite this, she sat beside him and returned the keycard to his free hand.

"Shh," Santoria softly spoke as her hand slowly took his, "I know you're upset with how things are going, Geine. And I'm sorry. But please, at least let me show you my sincerity."

"What? I don't get it…"

"You will, if you agree to come with me."

"Heh," Aurelio smirked, "Is this one of those *isekai* moments? Good one… I always knew you're some sort of anomaly in time-space specifically purposed to make my life worse…"

She squeezed his hand, "If that's what suits you to come with me, I'll accept it."

"Well, whatever. I'll soon wake up from this, right?"

"Who knows? Let's go, Geine."

She took the liberty to bring Aurelio's bag, if only because she saw how he was almost unable to drag himself to walk with her. Soon enough, they found themselves alone together in one of the hotel rooms. The exhausted writer collapsed on the bed without even changing or loosening his clothes. Santoria giggled as she tried to at least unbutton his long sleeve shirt.

"You see," she whispered as she snuggled beside him, "I've been meaning to say this for a long, long time… Now that we've gotten this far, honestly, I'm scared…"

"Mm-hmm…," Aurelio's response being indistinguishable from a common snort.

"Yes, yes… I always say I love you, but I guess you don't really know why… Let's just say, it's a meeting and a parting that you gave me. I can remember it like it was just yesterday. Anyway, what am I saying? You know what happened then, right? Let me get to the point…"

Before she mustered the courage to continue, she heard him snoring.

Santoria reached for his head, stroked his hair, and then upon slowly approaching even nearer, kissed him on the forehead, "You're right, this can wait. I'm just happy that at least, in your dreams, deep in your subconscious, I have a chance for you to accept me. To not unlove me."

For a while, after her short prayer, she waited if he would be talking in his sleep and probably betray some secrets. Unfortunately for her, those incriminating statements did not come. In reality, she could not get herself to fall asleep. Aurelio was now here with her. What a great opportunity! The possibilities were endless despite the short time they have, but what should she even do? Would it not jeopardize BIMMO 10314? The dynamics of relationships may have changed across time, but were the fundamentals quite the same since? Would this really be how to love in this New Normal?

Short Story by Jade Alipoon

Metronome

Eight billion people in the world. Eight billion hearts beating for someone.

These heartbeats have a different rhythm to follow and speed to catch up. Like a metronome. It depends on how we feel about the situation or the person we bonded with. It goes fast and goes normal, but on rare occasions, it goes rapidly and is hard to stop and we cannot even control them. Not you, not me, not everyone. As time passed, the beat begin to lose its rhythm. One year ago, you still feel butterflies in your stomach and later, you just felt empty and not contented at all. Realized that the rhythm of love can be stopped by pain and sadness and just like that, ended up broken. That is the musicology and wavelength of love for you, if you don't feel the same beat as someone, things get messy.

That was my love advice. And oh, by the way, I'm Chloe. My favorite class is Science and I'm an aspiring songwriter that is why I relate love to a metronome.

"Chlo, I heard from Chinchin you just turned down Marco. What happened?" That's my friend and seatmate in our Home Economics class, Pauline who is poking at my shoulder right now,

"I just don't feel him," I responded.

"What do you mean 'you can't feel him? He's a total package. He's a handsome, rich, and smart guy, and yet you rejected him?" Pauline was that persistent?

"That means she doesn't have any feelings for Marco, Paupau. You shouldn't force Chloe on him." Finally, Chinchin defended me.

"Fine. But don't just complain that she'll graduate single." Pau retorted.

"At least, I'm going to graduate with no regrets." I finally fought back at Pau.

I got home early. As soon as I opened the door of our house, mom and dad are now at the table for dinner. They're just waiting for me to join them on the food. Like anything usual, they ask me how was school and about my friends. While talking, I keep looking over my parents. Unlike present couples, they just look like they met for the first time on the first day of high school. Their wavelength, the chemistry of their love was still intact. Yung akin kaya kailan?

I finished all of my revisions tonight and am about to hit the bed. I looked up in the window to see the stars twinkling above the earth. Those starry boards— my moment got ruined by the annoying ringtone.

"H…hello?"

"Hi, is this Chloe Galvez from STEM Class A?"

"Yes, I am. Who is this?"

"This is Gian Carlo, from STEM Class B. I'm in a dire need of something."

"I see, like what?"

"Some of the lecture notes? Aren't we have the same teacher in that subject? Can you help me?"

"Oh… yeah, sure, tomorrow. In the library." I was hesitant at answering. Why? Cause of my heartbeat. It's starting to get faster. This was usually calm. Is this because of fear that Gian might do something bad? Or something like a flutter, because his voice sounds like music to my ears.

As I looked at myself in the mirror, I just found out that I am smiling. In my entire life, I haven't been smiling like this before because of a person. But what about the person I have never seen in my entire life who made me smile like this? Even at school? This is just the first time, Chloe. This is just the first time.

The next day, I went to the library to find Gian. And not for long, he was already there on the desktops.

By the looks of him, he is not the type of guy on the go. He was just an average-looking guy whom most girls would not go for him. But with his tan skin and well-fixed hair, I found him cute. Well, you can find guys attractive not in a romantic way. Except for my heartbeat which is now in the Vivace rhythm of a metronome.

"Kanina ka pa?"

"Ngayon lang. By the way, may iba kang kasama?" I asked.

"They are here but not with me. I told them that I'm waiting for someone." He smiled. His voice, his smile, but let's get into the real business here. I shared my notes with Gian and he shares something with his melodious voice. He was smart and articulate and within an hour, I am comfortable around him.

"By the way, thank you, Chloe. I can finally study with these notes." He thanked me and before I leave I handed him a flyer for our concert in the music club. "An invitation for you."

"Sorry Chloe, but I have bad ears for concerts." Feeling dejected, I lowered my head. "Hey, Chloe that doesn't mean your music sucks." He smiled at me while his hands cupped my cheeks. "I don't like going to concerts because I hate the crowd and very loud music." He explained. "But I'll visit you in the music club room." I thought he disliked music.

"Okay, Chlo. Can I start calling you Chlo?"

"It's okay. We're friends anyway" I smiled at him. "Take care of yourself eh?" Then he brought his bag and leave the library. While I am standing, smiling.

"Chlo? Earth to Chloe! What happened to you there?"

To my surprise, I'm gonna pull Chinchin's hair.

"Chinchin! Where did you come from?"

Chinchin grinned. "Nowhere. Then a little birdie witness someone who got shot by the cupid's arrow." She laughed as we got out of the library.

" Hey, don't make it an issue!"

"That was very strange of you, Chlo. If Pau was here, get your ears covered." She chuckles while getting my eyes rolling upward. Are they my friends?

Our first meeting with Gian will probably last.

Or so I thought?

Valentine's came and every girl in school is having flowers and chocolates in their arms. While others have their love letters on their desks and lockers. For those admirers who can only like someone but can't afford to make a move.

Rather than minding other girls' Valentine's presents, I went to the music room, and luckily, it was empty. Okay, I think Chloe the next Mozart will create new music to make everyone fall in love. Including Gian—wait, wait. He is not part of this. But he will be surely part of my listeners.

"Chlo, can you come with me to the park? It's like to have a mood for star gazing now." A message from Gian. When I looked through the window, the sun is about to set. I also read Chinchin's text that I skipped class. Oh, the horror of being in love. The feeling of Allegrissimo.

Hours later, I am now with Gian. Side by side, watching the stars. In silence.

"Gian?"

"Hmm?" He turned his head.

"Why did you take me here instead of your... you know..." I trailed off. I heard from Pau that Gian was kinda taken to Kathe, the pageant queen of our school from last year.

"Who, Kathe? She's my older sister. I already told her not to fetch me at school but dad is persistent. Anyway, why did you ask?"

Presto. My heart is in Presto. I don't know what to tell. "I just want to meet her."

"But not me?" He pouted, Stop it, you're cute already.

"Of course, I want to get to know you too. I haven't seen you in my entire life until last month." I replied.

"Then that's why we are here right now." He admitted. Vivacissimo.

"You're calling this a date?" And just like that he nodded. "We only met once." I was confused. I have to leave before things start to get awkward. "I... I have to go. My mom's waiting for me at home right now."

This isn't right. I'm confused, he's confused. I felt the rhythm, but not sure if his will sync with mine. Unrequited feelings are like injuries, they are common but they are painful.

During the following days, I was going with Chinchin and Pau. I haven't heard any news about Gian since he suddenly confessed to the park after I left him there. I know what I did was wrong but I don't want everyone to rush things. We met each other but I didn't want to say "hi" anymore. I don't want to explain my feelings to him anymore. At the same time, my heartbeat started to get back to Grave, calm and solemn. But something is missing.

I decide to go back to the music club room then I saw him again. I acted normal, walked straight, and say "hi" without clouded thoughts about what happened.

"What are you doing here?"

"To apologize."

"There's nothing to apologize, Gian—"Then he stood up only to hold me on the shoulders. "It's my fault."

"Don't blame yourself, Chlo."

Ugh, how could I avoid this feeling especially since my heart beats fast once more? It was already calm, and then another storm arrived.

"The truth is, I am afraid that… that…" I suddenly trailed off when I realized something. His heartbeat. It was in sync with him. Is this a sign or I'm getting my hopes high?

"That I never felt the same. I always missed you but I have no courage to say it." He added.

"I guess I shouldn't have left you that night," I whispered. "I thought you never liked me. And what you have said just left me confused." His arms allow me to hug him. I can feel his heartbeat. It's lively, happy, and fast. We're in sync.

"There's around eight billion different heartbeats in the world
But mine chose to sync up to yours
When we first met, I thought we'd never meet again
But here we are face to face on this starry board"

Once the rhythm was in sync with someone, this means this is a perfect sync to your heart. And Gian's heartbeat follows the same. It's not just how we feel, it's about how everything is perfect, like two metronomes playing at the same tempo.

Short Stories and Poem by Czarina Vaneza O. Dungca

Fell With Blue...

School is going to open tomorrow; my mind goes blank and all that concerns me is what will happen to us now. We are doomed, with no food left in the fridge but only leftovers and I still need to have repaired some stuff in the house – the door knobs that he had unscrewed to just get in, the wiring system that went awry, and, the tables and chairs he had torn apart.

Let's call it a day. I can't focus now and just stared blankly at the ceiling as I tried to catch some sleep.

And so, it goes, the night was merciless. And I just drowned myself in a crying spree while my kids are sleeping.

Was it just a few minutes ago and here I am sleepless, then it is already four am in the morning? And though my body aches I have to clean up the mess and then make breakfast for the kids.

My life had been this total mundane routine for those ten years. I do not even recognize the glory days I had before Pete came into my life. I was that youthful then, about to finish my Master's Degree, I have a promising career as a teacher, school paper adviser, and subject head in our department. But I have to leave all those behind to be with him. I left home with my old folks disagreeing with my decision to go to another place to reside with him there. Trade my job for another one in the local public school nearby and buy this house.

Then all I got are demeaning words, he squandered everything on gambling, women, and other vices. And when he is asked about his share in the household all those horrible years what I earn are insults and his dreadful fist.

As I look in the mirror, I ask myself what have I allowed him to do with me and the kids? It was all too much for the price I have to pay for choosing him. But no need for regrets, I have no time for that.

The kids went down, and hastily prepared for the day. They do not have a class yet as I enrolled them in a different school. I strived to send them to good schools apart from where I work, this is the only thing I could afford to give them. Especially Tin, because she is my eldest daughter. She has been our foremost casualty. I don't want her to suffer a similar fate as mine.

Enzo on one hand just turned five, and he will soon go to school like her elder sister next week. He has no clear idea of what happened between me and his father. He knows he is his father but has no deep feelings toward him because Pete is staying on and off with us. He was just like either a border, room renter, or visitor as Enzo perceives him. Not a father.

In a few minutes, their grandfather would come and fetch them. And here I am shuffling towards the bathroom to get myself ready. I also need to get to school really early and work on my computer and printer for not have a lesson plan yet.

I dressed up and put on my makeup too as if there are no traces of the horror that happened yesterday, I was the first one to open the faculty room door. While everyone is not yet around, I typed my lesson plan.

Around eight, colleagues have been filing into the faculty room and exchanged cheery greetings and some also greeted me. Good thing I finished my LP just in time so as not to be so obvious that I have just prepped it hours ago.

Then, there was this annual introduction of us with the new teachers and then with the rest of the student body. I saw two new male faculty members, one with thinning hair but with bushy eyebrows and then another one whose really tall, white complexioned, not so clear face but somehow not ugly or not superlatively good looking. I just stared.

But when their backgrounds were relayed to the group, oh well, they seem to be good fellows, especially with their craft. The first one was major in accounting and the other in computers. They are not from this city too but were hired anyway because much has to be filled in.

Days passed, so weeks, and months too. Other than school, I was able to have side hustles as a blog writer and a tutor.

Nothing much has been extraordinary for me except that I was able to go to and from school and the house. The kids are doing well so far in school and Tin has had a lot of achievements both academic and non-academic.

What about me? I have grown to improve both inside and out.

It was accidental that when I was with Pete I dyed my hair the wrong color exposing all the more the disparity of the roots and the old parts like a two-toned badly colored ombre. So, I chopped it off when the length was just enough for adapting a new color. Since I do not go out much and ride motorcycles like I did when Pete was here my complexion also improved. I also get to wear clothes and make-up I didn't wear before.

So much changed when Pete was gone from our home.

Between classes, how time flies that the first semester quickly ended. Who would have known that the second semester would now start? Oh, has it been like yesterday when I saw the two new male teachers? The almost thinning hair with bushy brows was Mr. Celdran and then the other one is Mr. Melvar the other one with a white complexion. They are from the graduating students while I was in the eleventh grade. Of, I will work with because the first one will soon be my leader in the Department because he was given that task. I don't mind really if he has the position I am fine with no ancillary position. I need side hustles and then take care of the kids also. The other one, I have to work with because he is the coordinator of anything that has to do with school records.

Mr. Melvar would still be a perennial workmate because later he would enroll his students in my class as they failed the previous semester. This one person had never been on my radar before, but as for the days that would roll by I would be ticked off by him.

Crush? No. I am too old for that. But I wonder, how so many of my female colleagues seem to be enamored by him. Okay, he has a nice chest and preferred body, but again for me, his face looks average. He rarely speaks, and when I get to log out or log in first we just nod our heads to each other as a fairly civil gesture of colleagues. Most times, he is snobbish. He would just ask for some information about his students taking my subject and would rush me into giving them grades. I hated that time when he asked for speedy computation because I was at home and sick.

Later, I told myself I will give him a code name so that when I am conversing with my friends at work about him it will not be obvious his favorite color - similar to the morning sky and the sea.

When I tell him to friends they were asking if I have a thing for him I told them no. I have been friends with males who are either former classmates back in the day and then would like to pursue me. No one, however, caught my attention yet. Maybe, I was just so afraid of commitment that my separation from

Pete is still in the works. Falling in love was the last thing of concern, but somehow…well, what if I feel that again? We'll see.

The Second Semester however ended too. Then the following two school years I managed to work full-time with the teachers of the graduating batch. I have no choice but to work with male teachers.

Mr. Melvar had been a constant sight lately. And we still do not talk much, but I do now with Mr. Celdran.

There are times that conversations had to be done with Mr. Melvar because I directly have to ask for assistance with the records. It was all just work.

One time I have to take a leave, an inopportune happenstance. Dad died. Mom and I would have to go run some errands in the supermarket -buy foodstuff for those who would be attending my father's wake.

Unaware of what is to come, and to whom I would meet in the supermarket it was the snobbish Mr. Melvar. Our eyes met, and both of us are startled. Because I never expected him to frequent supermarkets and though I am on bereavement leave I knew he should be in school for a seminar, which I was not able to attend because of my predicament. Him, I don't know.

So, I thought it was just that, but when mom and I finished purchasing groceries. I happen to see him again but, the goody two shoes Mr. Melvar was in a nearby barber shop to have his haircut. I could see that in the mirror he also saw me but he managed to ignore me.

I have to keep my dismay to myself because he never acknowledges me twice like I am not existing. But I have to let it pass because I have to be in the funeral chapel soon and when I get back to work I have to talk with him for some records again.

Oh no, it is Monday! Whether I like it or I don't I have to see Mr. Melvar. That crappy man! And this is it!

"Mr. Melvar, can I come in?" " Certainly Ms. Alviar, what Can I do for you." I was thinking about how to start my conversation with him as Mr. Celdran was also there, with peering eyes.

"I just dropped by because I have a few things to ask from you. The records of my two students and then I don't know exactly how to work things out with this online task for the filing of the records. Actually, I saw you last time but I guess it was quite off to speak with you because you are having your haircut ..."

It was quite awkward you know. But I continued with my speech although I am unsure why I was quite anxious, maybe because Mr. Celdran was there or the fact that the snobbish one asked me to sit next to him. Or do I look stupid with what I just said?

"Oh, you see, you just have to click this one so that the rest of the commands for filing could be done by you even if you are offline." And then he looked at me, I felt crazy warm.

I thanked him after, and then he said condolences to me. Right before I went out, I heard Mr. Celdran talk " Oh you have talked now to…" I felt embarrassed because I don't know if it is me, or that event in the supermarket and barbershop, or if it was all in my mind.

But a slew of happenings continued to arise, my encounters with Mr. Melvar.

He was a constant seatmate during seminars, and he could not be avoided by any means. There are happenstances where I really have to not avoid him.

But since that time, I do not know if my observations are valid but our eyes would always meet.

Can a single mom whose both penniless and depressed feel for someone? I do not know exactly.

Then our boss asked me to help him with a document to be submitted. Immediately, I went up to his room to ask. But for some reason, my eagerness was met with his blatant snobbish behavior.

"Oh, you don't have to do that Ms. Alviar, I can do it by myself. " I got furious because I felt embarrassed for being in such haste and then I was let down. Our boss told me that he, Mr. Melvar was asking for help. Then turns out that he didn't. So, I just looked in his eyes to make him feel that I think that it was more of his machismo talking and then a female colleague is to the rescue but he just refused.

His eyes are brown, but the pupils are not dilated. Me, psychoanalyzing him, that he is annoyed, mad, or just pesky. Then I felt myself suddenly going red, and instead of me becoming unperturbed I felt suddenly conscious. It has been years since I ever intensely looked into the eyes of a man.

Then he got also conscious and tried to look away, he began to stutter and I stepped back. I just sank onto the board with such embarrassment and cut the conversation. "Okay Mr. Melvar, I will go ahead but if you need anything I am just around." Awful like I am pleading. I went down like a dog with her tail in between her legs with a bowed head.

From there, we have been exchanging glances. He was across the faculty room, but I could sense he is looking at me. At times I tell myself, "Trina Alviar, get yourself together it might be your mind playing tricks on you. You are just hypersexual, delusional."

But why is my broken mind telling me, I am not, and also my heart? Oh my, my heart?

He would pass by my room like he was looking at me. I get nervous, I get excited. My heart flutters like that of a teenager.

But I constantly remind myself I can't fall for him. What about those female and gay teachers that are so attracted to him? And of course, I am a single mom. No one would take me seriously.

And him? I don't know if he would like me just the same. He has no ring yes....but some people say he is married and with kids.

And just like yes, as an adolescent female, I would try to get to know the person I like. I came to that point even looking at his social media profile but in vain with no answers, except for a few photos with two children and a woman. One or two articles of these.

I think I am trudging toward dark waters. I am liking a married man. Or more than that falling for him. Oh no. Please good heavens no. I do not know his real status. His feelings too. Not like this. Not trying to compromise my moral standing too.

Then instances do come to be with him because again I have to constantly check the files and records of my student with him. Can't really oh have a reason not to work with him. Darn.

"Ms. Alviar, you seem to forget the name of your students." He was smiling. " Sorry for that Sir, it might be a sign of aging that I am becoming oblivious to some details." He said in response "You don't look old, it's the other way around." Then he stood up, faced me, and was still chatting but his eyes are surveying me. I didn't want to melt but I cut off the conversation abruptly and thanked him and gave him chocolate for helping me out for the nth time. Motioned as well I gave others the same things when I ask for a favor. Then went out.

Then another incident ensued, this time the graduation picture taking of our students. He was there. I was fixing the collar of one student and then he approached "you are so lucky that your adviser does that to you…" I was tempted to look at him but I controlled the urge to do so. In the back of my mind, I was telling myself that what if I do that to him instead? And I just laughed.

I went out because I could feel my ears becoming quite warm in the guise of looking for other students who may not have their photos taken. Then students came flocking towards me and asked for a group selfie before entering the room where he was and the rest of the colleagues are taking pictures of their students too.

I saw him, and our eyes locked in a gaze again. I waved to a student from the inside but I also did to him.

Was it flirting? I don't know. It's been years since I felt butterflies in my stomach…behave Ms. Alviar.

Then another one, he cleaned up the chair for me in another meeting. He was right beside me again. But this time Mr. Celdran interrupted, and said to him "would you like to exchange places with me." This made me think. Was it already obvious that I like him? Or is he and his friends do know something I do not know…or is he trying to avoid me real soon? It made me panic and jittery.

I pretended not to know. Like I didn't care but chatted with a friend on the phone to distract me from the incident.

Rehearsals for the graduation came, a male student was chatting with me and he was just looking. Graduation happened too...

I went past them, Mr. Celdran and Mr. Melvar, the latter -he was so surprised to see me. The former told me "Wow, you look beautiful." I just said thanks. Mr. Melvar was smiling in amazement too. Then I just went to my room to wait for the arrival of my students, when I look back at them our eyes would meet again.

I don't know what is happening but... I think for me, it is not becoming healthy for me to have these feelings for him. I tell myself, convincing myself it might just be inside my head. I have to.

Then, another female colleague was teased by fellow teachers to him. I get jealous inside but who am I to feel that way? We had our faculty photo ops and then, I don't know if it was a ray of hope, we caught each other looking sneakily at each other.

But maybe, if it were true that there is something going on in there between me and him I don't know I can't tell. Those stolen glances, his nervous movements, him who cannot comprehend which way to go when I am around. Him looking at me from afar while I am talking with other male colleagues.

Is it just me or my little musings about him? Am I just lonely? I am just not that okay because I was left alone without any husband to take care of the kids with me, bills, and a lot more. Am I just looking for something to distract me and make the world feel less lonely?

So many questions. But as the days went by, I feel like we are both trying to avoid each other. I try not to be in the place where he is, I avoid going to the faculty room when I know he is around, and I would stay there when I can't see him. When I do, I pretend not to see him.

I think he is also doing the same. But what the heck, can the radio not play "Tonight" by FM Static while I staple test papers and he is passing by? Can he not look into my eyes? I am melting.

Can he not pass by the room trying to catch my gaze and then smile…? Because I am falling. Don't make me. Because we both know we can't. And You can't Mr. Melvar.

I know this has to stop, and so I waited for my turn in court to talk until I finished…anticipating the finality of the decision of my annulment. And to distract myself from ever thinking about Mr. Melvar, I trained myself to focus on my children. Even to apply abroad. In a few months, I will leave. And to Mr. Melvar, though I never disclosed how I feel. I am sure of what it is now, I love him.

Goodbye, and I love you Mr. Melvar. That every time you pass by, give me those glances I fall for you even more. And today, in my class as I teach my students for them not to try to keep those emotions in and face their own fears, here I am writing on the board and trying to focus on what I do, within me truly, I tell myself " Ms. Alviar, such a coward you are for not facing your own feelings for him…but courageous too because you have to put up with this every day knowing you love…" And there, as I look out the door, there was Mr. Melvar stopped right there and looking at me smiling. Waving a hand whose ring finger has a ring. He is as free as me. "Coffee, oh, your hyperacidity might kick in. A lesser evil option Ms. Alviar. Go out with me." I smiled back.

Hosea

"Oh my, I can't just leave..." She whispered to her choir mate sheepishly. As she was still in one of the rooms of the left wing of the university gymnasium waiting for the choir training to end for that day so she could go to the right wing where another meeting awaits.

She needs to stay a few minutes more as she is one of the leaders of the Sopranos, there will be a huge cultural and talent showcase event where the big names in the region would be there to perform like local poets, string quartets, theatre groups, etc. She will be singing the solo part of one of the songs in the chorale repertoire. Plus, she needs to help out new recruits to master the song lineups.

Ten minutes of overtime and she flew out of the room to hastily walk to the right wing. Luckily only a few student journalists like her are there and the writing workshop facilitator got caught up in an engagement prior to the event; unfortunately got stuck in bottleneck traffic along the way so there is still some time to subtly comb her hair with her fingers as she noticed that her hair looked quite horrible perhaps gathering all of it into a dirty bun would do the trick.

At the corner of her eye right around her left side, she noticed someone is looking at her and she glanced back at him. His shoulders are very broad, he had a bit of burnish complexion but was nevertheless handsome and his lips especially the lower half were plump for a kiss and his eyes were not rounded but similar to her doe eyes.

The charmer seems familiar; he looks like her childhood crush Aaron. So, she hatched a plan of approaching him after the workshop. It ended but the guy just simply vanished perhaps he was catching up on his class that afternoon.

When will be the next journalism workshop? Well, it would be a week from now. Maybe then she will be able to confirm if he is her long-time crush or otherwise.

She then went to a mad dash towards her afternoon class as well before the English Professor closes the door.

But she cannot shake him off her mind; she mumbled "will he recognize me? Is he Aaron or just a figment of my imagination? Or there is just an uncanny semblance between them?"

Maybe, the much-anticipated discovery will be next week nonetheless.

That week came and finally even if the guy belongs to a different student publication he sat beside her. He asked her name and introduced himself. "Hi, by the way, I have seen you last week. I wanted to talk to you but I still have my class after the workshop. So, I thought perhaps, next time I would have the opportunity to get to know you. I am Hosea from Savant Society."

"Oh, I am Dionne; I am a News Editor from Onomatopoeia the College Education's official publication. What's your position?"

"I am a photojournalist. Are you a newbie or a veteran?"

"Hmm, I am a newbie modesty aside; it was actually quite serendipitous to be a part of the newspaper team. I just went with my friend and the proctors of the examination told me why not try out and give it a shot or take the test since it would take long before everyone finishes…and here I am."

"Wow, that is awesome! I tried out for the newspaper because I want to be active on a lot of things…ummm I am also in theatre, even cooking I am an HRM student. One time will you watch our stage play?"

"Okay then. If time permits, I will."

The facilitator entranced the room and everyone was silent. He isn't Aaron but it is a privilege to get to know someone who is also new when it comes to writing for student publications.

While slides are being presented on the white screen and the facilitator was discussing something about writing effective Editorials, Dionne can't help but look at her new buddy. Surprisingly, he too is gazing at her.

She felt a jolt from her spine crawling towards the whole of her perplexed if she has something dangling from her nose or her hair again in disarray making her blush. Those eyes spoke to her despite the darkness of the room and the silence that enveloped all of them in attendance - like it was just them and nobody else and the rest are just part of the backdrop.

Then the facilitator asked him, what is his idea about an editorial he valiantly responded "it is the part of the newspaper that highlights the stand of the whole team regarding a certain, timely issue" and all applauded.

Whew at least it was not her; she and he almost laughed because apparently, they were caught having a world of their own.

The following week was the last leg of the writing workshop and she thought they might not see each other again. But she was hopeful that he will text her that night.

"Till next week, hoping to see you again," Hosea told her and they walked side by side. Their hands brushed onto each other like there was a static force that binds them momentarily, hopefully, a bit longer.

Will he make that text message? Will he call her? After supper she went to her room cleaned up, bathed, and read her books for tomorrow's Preliminary Exams. And it was past nine in the evening but there was no call or text.

She said her prayers and was about to lie down on her bed when suddenly her phone rang. Finally, sickles of hope came flooding her. A wide grin came across her face and the anticipation responding to the call.

Yes, it is him! But, "Dionne..." he said in an almost inaudible voice. I would not be able to finish the writing workshop next week. We have rehearsals for our theatre play. But can you please claim my certificate on my behalf? I already spoke to the Students' Services Office about it and they agreed since we will be staging the play real soon in the university and outside of it too, they say in the nearby town as well."

"Okay, no worries. Just give me your picture, have someone take it so I would at least have an idea how someone as handsome as you perform."

Ooopss that was quite awkward why did she say that? She felt her cheeks burn in sheer embarrassment as if only the beddings could engulf her, may it be.

Hosea let out a thunderous laugh, and said "Oh, you find me handsome? No one ever told me that?"

"Hmmm, why not you're my friend. Are we? Yes, we are?"

"Will we remain that?" And sparks flew all night long. Hope little by little pries the door open.

***

He was never able to attend indeed and that whole day his phone was left unattended. He might be so busy to even pick it up. Dionne then resorted to musing at the fact that he isn't that boy Aaron from elementary days they might have looked similar in some aspects but he is far more genial than him and could be a good friend but at the back of her mind she desires for something else being his girl.

But how could that be if she is three years older than him? Would it not hinder them to understand each other? Or is there a chance that Hosea would like him back?

After the series of journalism writing workshops the semester ended in a flash, they continued texting each other but still, they would not admit to each other.

Then the two weeks came for duty for publication booths where they have to collect from fellow students the publication fee and distribute the remainder of unclaimed newspapers.

During the first day, Hosea was not there and Dionne was quite sad to abate boredom while waiting for students to come by, she and one of the staffers sang while the other played the guitar. The day ended but no signs of Hosea.

The next day, early morning Hosea was not yet around and during the lunch break Dionne took her lunch at their student publication office while the staffers went out to buy their meal from a nearby mall. The gravy of the chicken spilled onto her white blouse. "Dammit!" She said she was not bringing an extra shirt. Then somebody knocked on the door, it was the usual cheery Hosea.

He saw that her blouse was stained with gravy; he looks obviously straight out of the shower and smells of a mix of earthy and herby-toned cologne. He took off his shirt and gave it to Dionne and brought out of his backpack a bomber jacket with a zipper.

"We had a very tiring last-day rehearsal, it seems like bringing extra clothes is a good option. I sneaked into the athletes' bathroom to take a shower so when I visit you here I would smell like a baby. But it seems like you are the one needing a spare shirt and you cannot just return to the booth looking less flashy."

She was peering slightly at his brazen but well-sculpted upper torso and that abs it made her face burst red. And Hosea just smiled at her. When she gained her composure, she excused herself to change her top with his.

When Dionne came back she invited him to go to their respective booths to render their usual duty.

While rendering their few hours before closing the booths Dionne told Hosea that he actually looked like Aaron. "Who is he "he muttered. "He is a childhood friend, crush. But then again please ummm…" He interrupted "It's all right; you look amusing and cute with your constant blushing." She tried to change the topic by saying "you are my lucky charm; finally, I could close the booth earlier than usual, after a long day." She gestured that there are only a few staffers who had helped out and that she is greatly thankful for him, his company, and his assistance especially since the Editor-in-Chief is not also around. Then later, he asked if he could call him "Charm". She accepts and he showed her, that he had named her in his phone contacts.

Around 3:00 pm in the afternoon, there are no more students going to the booths but they still have an hour before going home.

"Hey! You okay?" Hosea asked jokingly at her. "Hmmm, ah yes. You are talking to me?"

"Who is that lucky guy you are daydreaming about?" "Do I look like daydreaming to you?" Dionne defensively said.

"Okay then, if it is all right I would like to give you my schedule for the next Semester. And I would like to have yours too."

"Your classes are in the morning and afternoon, while mine is mostly afternoon and evening…well don't you think that is a hassle for you?"

"No, I insist that I would like to give mine and take yours. If I need to sit in one of your classes I will."

"What's that?" asked Hosea as her belly furiously grumbles. "'You hungry, let's look for some grub downstairs?"

He took her hand and everyone is looking at them Dionne put away his hand, stooped then spoke to one of her two staffers. "Please, look at my stuff I will be back soon."

"What is our first stop?" asked Dionne. "Very well have you forgotten, as I have said cafeteria first? Then, ahhh, we'll figure out where would be next since there are only a few or none at all who come to our respective booths."

So, Hosea and Dionne had light snacks downstairs and chatted for a few minutes more to kill time. They munched on some potato crisps and chocolate oatmeal cookies and drank soda water too.

He then asked for one more favor which is to come with him to their college building where their office is. He motioned that a few stacks of newspapers are still in his locker. It is open because some people are also there. And when they are there he started acting seriously.

How can a guy be both so intelligent and kind could also be this quite a looker? And thinking about having this young man for a boyfriend could be quite a long shot. But she just looked at him while he removed the stack from the locker.

She had her loves before but they all ended in misery, and the constant presence of her mother and a reminder to pursue a career in journalism would confront her every single day.

But every time she wants to keep such thoughts at bay she is lured toward him; her mind wanders off to Hosea. She constantly imagines how it would feel if he would be her future husband and what their offspring would look like.

"

"What's your favorite song?" he asked. "Hmmm, "'We are one'. The song we previously learned from training." "Can you sing it for me" "Okay then…"

"What's yours? " "I just heard this song these past few days on the radio but the lyrics say, "I think I'm falling…falling…in love…"

"All right, seems it would rain if you would continue singing let's go."

***

"The remaining stack of newspapers in my locker…umm here it is now. Would you mind helping me out there?"

"Sure, that's fine"

Once they are outside of the office, he suddenly said to her "Please don't get mad if I would tell you something."

Her heart is raising thinking that he might have sensed that she has this certain fondness for him. And that she might get rejected even without telling him of her feelings.

"I hope you would not get offended if….I think I like you, no…I love you already." She got stunned and do not know how to respond.

A sudden adrenaline rush came to her, and maybe courage as well to tell him she feels the same. But before she would actually say her thoughts one of the staffers appeared out of nowhere and approached her. He mouthed that in a few minutes' time, they will be closing the booth since it is 3:45 pm already.

She assured the staffer she would catch up and that she even mentioned that they could close the booth now. That he has nothing to worry about because she has a spare office key, she instructed the staffer to take her stuff to the office. But a few seconds before the staffer turned away she changed her mind and told him to leave her things at the booth instead.

Once the staffer is gone they both sat down on a concrete bench nearby and returned to the conversation. "So, what would it be then for both of us? Are you my girlfriend now?" relayed Hosea.

"It is quite fast and I am two years older than you…my schedule and yours are not the same too."

"I do not care much about your age and our schedule what I know is that I love you. I love you."

"I feel the same. But if I give my heart to you, please do take care of it."

They returned to their booths, the room is locked and no one is there everyone went home already. Then they went to Dionne's office but when she is about to get the key from her purse she realized the key is also left at the booth together with her bag.

They just laughed and Hosea told her that as her boyfriend now she would take her to her home since her parents might worry.

"Mom is waiting for me; Dad is no longer with us for three years now." "I am sorry to hear that…"

"No worries because we know he is okay up there you know."

They went to his office again luckily one staffer is there and his backpack was taken there too. And from there they walked to the university parking lot when he stopped in front of a red shiny car. He took out from his pocket seemingly alarm and keys to the vehicle and invited her in.

While driving he took her hand and kissed it. "From now on, I will be your personal chauffeur and I will see to it that you are always safe."

Dionne kissed his forehead and he went on driving until they reached her abode.

From there she ushered him in and introduced him to her folks, cousins, and the whole clan but in particular her mother. Malia her mother succinctly asked some questions about his background and with the looks of it somehow, she is impressed that he came from a good family, he is excellent in class, and has a lot of talents too.

She dished out for them Dionne's favorite crabs with a sauce made from tomato sauce, crab roe, garlic, and butter plus there is ice cream for dessert. Hosea is delighted that it so happened that he too likes those crabs.

He stayed an hour more with Dionne they sat on the wicker sofa on the veranda before him going ahead. There he just caressed her hair and grasp her hand. And they were just looking into each other's eyes without a word but knowing what their hearts are saying.

He then reclined on her lap closed his eyes and said "I wish this would be forever. I am happy to be with you always."

She then took one of his hands and placed it on her chest where he could feel her heartbeat. And she likely said" I love you, I haven't been this happy for ages…I wish I could keep you forever."

"What should we say to our peers tomorrow? How can we explain to them that we got left behind because I said yes to you?"

"Oh well let them assume that now we are together. Actually, one of them asked me if we are an 'item' and I said yes."

'Why did you say that? I just said yes today." "Maybe because I prayed really hard that my wish would come true and it did. I just said it to him in advance."

"Oh, you! You are such a bad boy!" "No, I am not…I am just swept away by you the moment I first saw you."

"What about me being older than you?" "For now, let us not think about that what is important is that you are my girlfriend."

He looked away to take a glimpse of the time and it is 9:30 pm, how time flies! He told her that he must go and she walked with him towards the gate.

He paused for a while and stared at her. It might be that since they are already together she must give her a resounding goodbye. He was 5'9" and she was 5' and so she tried her hardest to reach at least his cheek and plant him a kiss. But Hosea was thinking to kiss her instead on the lips, and so he did.

It may seem quite hasty, but it was not just a smack he opened his mouth to graze hers. For her, it tasted not of crabs but of Double Dutch ice cream her mother offered him.

She kissed her back though at first, she was quite shy and closed her eyes. But suddenly there are footsteps from behind it could be Malia and they unlatched themselves from that passionate kiss. "Good night love, "said Dionne. "I love you Dionne" are his words before he got into his car.

I, The Once-Fallen Lover

It could be that I always accompany my cousin as she watches those cheesy teeny-bopper shows during the '90s that I had developed this distorted fantasy about love. And as I often hear her stories about her crushes and how she describes them to me there was this ideation that the end all and be all of being is finding that someone who could make you complete.

I carry on this until my prime years; I saw myself as a game player and though the stakes are high I mostly gamble with my all. And exactly, the end of each game is predictable. I lose.

Now that I am in my late 30s around two years from now entering the glorious age of forty I think to myself I have learned the hard way. Not just bruises and concussions but I burned myself in the process.

In my mid-20s I met my future husband who is now my ex-husband and he thought me the most potent lesson I could ever have.

I could speak about him with an adamant tone as I come to realize that one day you are too in love with the person and built your dreams around him because it felt so right. Me and him against the world, everything was blissful despite the numerous red flags. Then you just give up on him because there was nothing to gain except two young children that came out from me.

I wasted ten long years, of my youth and traded my ambition because I loved him and thought we have the same thinking that we would have a family of our own.

I unfurled this wrongful perception of him and it might have been that he was the one. I felt free, that once in my life I could be just myself and not pretend to be anyone. I have always been that insecure woman who never looked straight in the mirror and not found herself beautiful.

Not that I never had suitors or boyfriends before him, but I constantly have that need for validation from people outside of me. I am a foreigner to the concept that I am worth it. Maybe it was that child within, that needs to heal, and that little one that would be the butt of jokes because I was petite, too thin, geeky type, and introverted. Well, if you would put me together with my cousins I would be that sore thumb sticking out. As with my friends especially during high school, I am noticeably the small one, a private pun I am the mascot of the gang.

Another rickety sense of self I have is that I may have had relations with other guys but most are short-lived. The fact then that I have to juggle studies, being sort of a working student rather trainee for non-academic scholarship and academic scholar as well made me so pressured that stick thin I study all day and all night.

And the casualty was my social life and my personal relationships. As for consolation, maybe not second best in the eyes of my parents nothing else.

I have met good men worthy of marriage but I was so afraid I could not measure up because they might be too good for me. Or if someone barges in and pursuit me I try to hide away my feelings toward them.

I prayed hard that the idealized version of matinee idols in shows my cousin and I watched would barge out of the television set and be right in front of me the soonest.

Then, with the awful twists and turns of faith, he came. He did not come in a sort of imaginary box with a big bough. I didn't like him because he was boorish, rough on the edges, a lady's man even a gigolo as words of mouth would have it. But I fell for him anyway, because he was the only one that was there when I was struggling with health issues and when I felt unloved by those people who should be there for me at my darkest.

I thought it was love…especially on his part. But his tears were just, crocodile tears, his compassion was just for the show. His sort of love was just manipulation. His fake emotions I paid for dearly as I am on the brink of personal depletion. The words I love you do not make sense anymore as they have been said by him to countless women he openly tells of his indiscretions.

Who would have thought that there would be days I would be filled with bruises? At one point, a hand was almost smashed. A spirit that was ultimately crushed, self-esteem and worth that I could not mend, and for the record deeply thrown in the dumps.

I am so, broken, I cannot look in a mirror literally because I felt uglier than I was before. With a baby in my tummy and a body weight plummeting to eighty pounds hanging on to life and trying to keep the little person inside of me alive. Then, on one hand, a five-year relying on me to be strong.

Then, I just woke up. Realizing enough. I can't do it anymore. And the years of self-doubt I finally muster the courage to break away.

In truth, there are no knights in shining armor. Well, as a history teacher there aren't any anyway – but those who wet their trousers because they can't run away easily, those that have knocked off teeth, those that don't shower most times, and those with horrendous breaths pages of history books and research could attest to.

Mine was a filthy knight. A man with no soul, no real emotions for anyone but a master of himself. Throws himself into the arms of other women. Find satisfaction in self-deprecating pleasures.

However, though it was a painful realization that the dream was not actually a fairy tale but a horrid nightmare I awaken just in time…before it was too late.

I ran as far as I could where he could no longer reach for me. And in that abysmal darkness where I thought I would never be able to go out, I managed to escape slowly.

In that love game, I took a bet and lost big time. But on the other hand, I won. I was able to take over the reins of my life. I am painstakingly starting from scratch.

But as I look at the faces of my children, there is this redemptive value that I affirm to myself that it was still worthwhile to live. As for the love I have hankered and yearned for, from shadows and figments of characters of teen-oriented shows they weren't for real. You could not make a real man carved out from them because they are works of fiction. In real life, the love that I long for is in those little ones that I walk hand in hand with every day, those whose arms draped around my waist and at times caress my face. That kind of love I may not win me a potential lover, with me not wanting it anymore. But the love is so pure from my children is no less. Enough to make me whole again. Reason to look forward to waking up every single day.

Hey Muse…Your Eyes

You confuse me

But at the same time, you make me feel alive

Despite the darkness, I am in

You make the day light up

Should it be that I should not catch or harbor feelings for you?

Because you can't be mine

And with the circumstances that we both have

The world where we both trudges may be the same

But the priorities we set are somehow different

Unspoken words, melting moments, accidental touches

Frequent encounters, and pleasantry we share

Or maybe those stolen glances, times we caught each other looking

I am just fine with them… I can't just ask for anything that is beyond those

Or should I?

I tried many times to convince myself that I should do whatever

To kill these emotions, grapple with them with all my might

Put me back together and remove me from this situation where I am stuck with the thoughts of you

But then, how can I move on when exactly just a whiff of your scent takes me to another world

That your presence makes me tremble and shiver

That when I am left with you my insides are clashing

What hurts, I guess that if I get jealous

What if I start missing you

That is when my thoughts wander out there to you

There is no effect whatsoever on you because I am just a ghost

You don't- can't and won't fathom the gravity

The extent to which I want you for myself badly

The ache of imagining that I could at least embrace you

The entangling musings or of wishing I could tell you

And the solace I have is to pen all these on paper

I can't go further…

My male muse I would just paint you…

Because your eyes and mine meet

I hanker to cross the line

So long as I could keep mum about you and this love

I will, just let me revel in the contemplation of you tonight…

Poems by
Marjorie Sirah San Miguel

Spaces

It is honestly a grotesque feeling,
To be wanting to be with you
But can't;
And the only way to surpass that,
Is if I close my eyes
And let the night
Take me to you instead.

Us

I love you in ways that I know
And only understand—
And I am still learning
The language your soul speaks,
And the rhythm your heart beats,
While also tuning in my own tempo.

Nemis

I am still learning about all that is you;
and the more I do, the less afraid I become
in the idea of being vulnerable with someone,
and diving in too deep;

I hope you don't mind me take my sweet time
familiarizing the person that you are,
until my heart knows that it's safe
to make a shelter out of yours.

11:11

I don't think it was the timing that was bad,
No, not even the crossed-out stars in the sky
During those sleepless nights filled with you –
But the long pauses it took before realizing
The possibility of you and me.

Darling, you were a good dream.

Dream Catcher

I fell in love with a daydreamer
And a night thinker;
And I am not sure how to live a life
That's both fantasy and reality all at once.

Museum Full of Scars

I wonder if you'd still be able to look at me with love
And touch me with tenderness if one day I decided
To undress my soul and reveal my raw, naked self;

Showing all imperfections that have scarred my being;
The ugly and unlovable parts I have buried deep within,
And have kept hidden from this cruel world—

I wonder if you'd still love me regardless.

Unrequited

I love you from afar;
Undeniably,
Consistently
Irrevocably—
Always have
And always will

Defying every star
And repainting
The night sky;
But in real life,
You won't ever
Know me still

For I am a walking scar,
Existing only to hide
Every inch of my
Identity—

And in time, I hope to be;
Afraid not to conceal.

About the Authors

Triscia Mae Abe

Triscia Mae Abe with the pen name of eut_channn (yu_channn) is a lazy girl with a huge dream. She loves watching anime and her favorite anime of all time is One Piece and she loves Zoro the marimo. She speaks what's on her mind but often gets misinterpreted, that's why sometimes she chooses silence. She loves Saitama, the bald main character in One Punch Man a lot, just like how she loves cats.

Maria Cristina Gornez

Maria is currently studying for her master's degree in literature while working as a broker support online for an outsourcing company engaged in the Australian Insurance industry. This would be the first time that she submitted her work due to a lack of confidence. She finds writing a poem too difficult but ends up expressing her feelings through a poem. She's always in awe of how poets can weave captivating words into a poem. As a beginner, she finds it entertaining to write a narrative poem. Reading a story in a rhythm makes her smile, and she hopes to share this feeling with her readers.

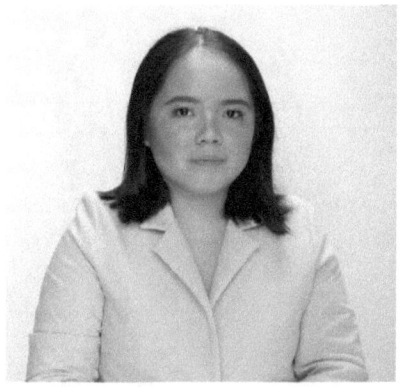

Bhon Glory Jayn P. Cabilete

Bhon Glory Jayn P. Cabilete is a first-year BA in Literary and Cultural Studies student at the University of San Carlos. She is the current script writer of Dear Tita Mercy (DTM), a radio program by the Cebuano Studies Center (CSC), Department of Communications, Linguistics, and Literature, (DCLL), and Pulong sa mga Alagad sa Obra (PALABRA) aired by DYRF 12.15. Her first novel, *Dwell with Snaedis*, is published under Paperink Publishing House. Now, she's a freelance writer in various writing platforms such as Amazon Kindle Vella under the pseudonym of PURPLE GLORY. She's currently on-lookout with literature-related opportunities and areas of improvement similar to writing in different genres, styles and types.

Chantel Ruecille C. Bargamento

Chantel Bargamento has been writing for Horizon Publishing since October 2022 and has published four on-going serial stories under them. She also likes composing songs during her free time.

Golden Rose

Golden Rose is a young writer entering the world of authors. She has been writing since she was 11 years old. Writing is her biggest passion; she has been writing scripts, stories, and songs, none of which are known to the public due to her low self-esteem. But as the new year began, she slowly got out of her comfort zone and began showing what she was capable of. One of her goals in life is to be a successful author, which starts now as she takes her passion out into the world to be read and heard by others.

Arius Lauren Raposas

With a heart to honor God and the people, Arius Lauren Raposas has faithfully served in the executive and the legislative branches of government in the Philippines. He finished a bachelor's degree in history (magna cum laude) and a master's degree in public administration (thesis track) at the University of the Philippines Diliman. Besides his public service and academic contributions, he has authored a number of literary works through the years, a roster that includes *Code Antony* (2010), *Run to the Sky* (2017), *Countdown to Inferno* (2020), Kotabahara: The City of God (2020), Muni: Dream Princess (2020), *Revolution: 80 Days* (2022), and this story you now possess. He has shared knowledge related to his expertise through national and international media appearances. Also, he has established a presence in social media, where his history website called Filipino Historian (2012) has already reached millions of people.

Jade Alipoon

Jade Alipoon, also known as "ancheeeyooo," is a fiction writer from Naval, Biliran. She is a graduate of Bachelor In Secondary Education major in English in Biliran Province State University and a campus journalist for three years. She found happiness in writing and believes that her works can create significance to everyone—including herself. Out of her fanfiction shadows, she is ready to craft her own work in the next level.

Czarina Vaneza O. Dungca

Czarina is a fervent reader of Paulo Coelho and Nicholas Sparks' works. Her premiere motivator was her friend Jayann; she constantly visits her during college days and she encourages her to write. To this day, Czarina pens about love, which perhaps eludes her and her dear friend Jayann, and all works are dedicated to her as she reads them in heaven and all those lovers who just passed by and made an impact on both their lives.

Marjorie Sirah "Sai" San Miguel

Marjorie works in the recruitment industry; a writer and digital artist during her free time. She has published a short story during her college days that was titled "Si Putol at Ako", and was then chosen by her professor in Filipino to be set forth in the school library. She's also an animal advocate, believing that every animal, no matter what breed, deserves a loving shelter. She fosters her rescues until she finally finds a "furever home" for them as she likes to call it. One of her rescues is a cat named Karma, that she found outside her home.

www.ingramcontent.com/pod-product-compliance
Lightning Source LLC
LaVergne TN
LVHW091632070526
838199LV00044B/1029